# FALSE DAWN

## SGT RAKESH SIYAL
### BOOK TWO

## ED JAMES

Copyright © 2024 Ed James

The right of Ed James to be identified as the author of this work has been asserted in accordance with the Copyright, Designs and Patents Act 1988. All rights reserved.

No part of this publication may be reproduced, stored in or transmitted into any retrieval system, in any form, or by any means (electronic, mechanical, photocopying, recording or otherwise) without the prior written permission of the publisher. Any person who does any unauthorised act in relation to this publication may be liable to criminal prosecution and civil claims for damages.

This is a work of fiction. Names, characters, businesses, places, events and incidents are either the products of the author's imagination or used in a fictitious manner. Any resemblance to actual persons, living or dead, or actual events is purely coincidental.

Cover design copyright © Ed James

# OTHER BOOKS BY ED JAMES

### DI ROB MARSHALL SCOTTISH BORDERS MYSTERIES

Ed's first new police procedural series in six years, focusing on DI Rob Marshall, a criminal profiler turned detective. London-based, an old case brings him back home to the Scottish Borders and the dark past he fled as a teenager.

1. THE TURNING OF OUR BONES
2. WHERE THE BODIES LIE
3. A LONELY PLACE OF DYING
4. A SHADOW ON THE DOOR
5. WITH SOUL SO DEAD
6. HIS PATH OF DARKNESS
7. FEAR OF ANY KIND (early 2025)

### SGT RAKESH SYAL POLICE THRILLERS

1. FALSE START
2. FALSE DAWN
3. FALSE HOPE (coming 2025)

FALSE START is a prequel novella to the Marshall series and is available for **free** to subscribers of Ed's newsletter or on Amazon:

Sign up at https://geni.us/EJLCFS

## POLICE SCOTLAND

Precinct novels featuring detectives covering Edinburgh and its surrounding counties, and further across Scotland: Scott Cullen, a rookie eager to climb the career ladder; Craig Hunter, an ex-squaddie struggling with PTSD; Brian Bain, the centre of his own universe and bane of everyone else's.

1. DEAD IN THE WATER
2. GHOST IN THE MACHINE
3. DEVIL IN THE DETAIL
4. FIRE IN THE BLOOD
5. STAB IN THE DARK
6. COPS & ROBBERS
7. LIARS & THIEVES
8. COWBOYS & INDIANS
9. THE MISSING
10. THE HUNTED
11. HEROES & VILLAINS
12. THE BLACK ISLE
13. THE COLD TRUTH
14. THE DEAD END

Note: Books 2-8 & 11 previously published as SCOTT CULLEN MYSTERIES, books 9-10 & 12 as CRAIG HUNTER POLICE THRILLERS and books 1 & 13-14 as CULLEN & BAIN SERIES.

## DS VICKY DODDS SERIES

Gritty crime novels set in Dundee and Tayside, featuring a DS juggling being a cop and a single mother.

1. BLOOD & GUTS
2. TOOTH & CLAW
3. FLESH & BLOOD
4. SKIN & BONE
5. GUILT TRIP

### DI SIMON FENCHURCH SERIES

Set in East London, will Fenchurch ever find what happened to his daughter, missing for the last ten years?

1. THE HOPE THAT KILLS
2. WORTH KILLING FOR
3. WHAT DOESN'T KILL YOU
4. IN FOR THE KILL
5. KILL WITH KINDNESS
6. KILL THE MESSENGER
7. DEAD MAN'S SHOES
8. A HILL TO DIE ON
9. THE LAST THING TO DIE
10. HOPE TO DIE

### Other Books

Other crime novels, with *Lost Cause* set in Scotland and *Senseless* set in southern England.

- LOST CAUSE
- SENSELESS

# CHAPTER ONE

Sergeant Rakesh Siyal clutched the top strap of his rucksack, running the fabric against his skin. Still light in the sky, considering it was the last day in November. St Andrew's Day, Scotland's national day. Rakesh didn't think it had any military overtones or meaning. Nationalistic ones, sure, and lots of haggis and whisky, neither of which he liked.

A gang of neds marched along the pavement like they were going to war.

Not his problem. Yet.

He sat back in the passenger seat and watched Peffermill Road whizz past in a blur. Edinburgh University's playing fields lurking behind a low-slung row of American buildings: modern flats that looked like a motel on Route 66, a Honda motorbike garage, a Triumph one. Then on past the new property developments that must've popped up one time when he'd blinked, past the Nairn's oatcake factory, which always smelled glorious.

He dropped his bag back into the footwell and let out a deep breath.

Afri looked over at him. 'That was a fairly serious sigh there. You okay?'

Rakesh liked her being behind the wheel – made him feel safe and secure. He swallowed down another breath. 'Not really.'

A smile passed across her lips. 'Just one more shift, then you're off for four days, right?'

'Right, but try telling that to my brain at midday when I'm supposed to be asleep.' The sigh slipped out of his lips. 'Anyway. You're right. Get through this, get some sleep, then we can have a fun weekend.'

'Well, what's left of one. It's Saturday, after all.'

'Is it?' Rakesh laughed, but the truth was he was worried about what these shift patterns were doing to his brain. 'Finish at three. I'll get up at nine and try to jerk my body clock back to normal. Okay?'

'If you're sure...' Afri turned left, then pulled into the car park in front of Craigmillar police station.

The modern building basked in the last of the afternoon's crisp sunshine, looking more like a library or a primary school. 'Modern' was doing a lot of work there – it must be pushing thirty years old – but still. Maybe that was the whole point: it could be converted pain-free when

Police Scotland needed to sell it off, unlike other buildings full of asbestos and that concrete that crumbled.

Afri stopped in front of the station and leaned over to kiss him on the mouth. Her lips tasted of fresh strawberries. 'How long left until you're back in the Borders?'

Rakesh sat back and ran a hand through his hair. 'It was supposed to be for a month, but that was two months ago. So who knows...'

'And then you'll be back in the Borders?'

Rakesh nodded. 'Back being a detective.'

Afri sat back, arms folded. The engine still thrummed. 'Do you trust him?'

'Rob?' Rakesh got a nod, then gave her a shrug in return. 'I've no reason not to.'

She looked away. 'I learned to trust nobody.'

'I'll try not to take that personally.'

Afri reached over and stroked his hair. 'Present company excepted.'

Rakesh took her hand and kissed it. Then felt the strain of another sigh climbing his gullet. 'Guess I better get this over with, eh?' He reached over to return her kiss. 'Enjoy the ceilidh tonight. Wish I was coming.'

She laughed. 'I don't understand any of the dances.'

'I don't think anyone does, but they just throw each other around.'

She smiled at that. 'I'll try to have fun. Then I'll have a good sleep while you work.'

Rakesh leaned over for a final kiss. 'Goodnight.'

'Goodnight, Rakesh. See you in the morning.'

He got out of the car and lugged his backpack across to the station entrance. He stopped and watched her battered old Mazda drive off. A heaviness tugged at his shoulders, like a giant was squashing him into the ground. He wrapped his backpack over both shoulders, then slipped in through the station entrance.

The wide reception area was quiet for once, despite it being Saturday afternoon, just the desk clerk scratching his pencil off a book of puzzles. He looked up at Rakesh, gave a nod, then went back to it.

Rakesh opened a door at the side, then walked through into the corridor that smelled of mushrooms and regret. He nudged open the door to the sergeants' locker room, trudged in and dumped his bag on the wooden bench. He sat down and stared into space.

He had over an hour to get his squad ready for back shift. All those tasks they needed to follow up, not to mention the new ones passed to them by day shift, who would still be out and about, hunting and searching and following up. Hibs were away today, so football policing wasn't their responsibility.

Afri was right – get through this, then he could sleep that horrible half a night that battered his body clock back to something approaching normality. And hopefully he could enjoy a bright, crisp Sunday somewhere with her. And it wouldn't take so much coffee to end up ruining tomorrow night's sleep too.

Rakesh got up and walked through to the toilet. He was unbuckling his belt when he spotted it – just a brown cardboard tube where a fluffy white roll of toilet paper should be.

'Bloody hell.' He charged out of the sergeants' room, then opened the next door.

The constables' locker room was much bigger. The stinging body spray shrouded six male officers in various stages of undress in a thin mist.

In the middle, a wannabe alpha male was holding court. Tall and athletic, unbuttoning his denim shirt. PC George Bell. One of those cops who wasn't so much Rakesh's responsibility as inevitably his fault. 'I mean, it's what happens when you take the Saudi money, right? Don't know what's happening to the sport.' He flicked his shirt off. 'A lot less honour in boxing these days. Different from when I fought, back in the day.'

Rakesh stepped into the room.

He got a nod from a tall cop in a black 'GANGSTER' T-shirt. 'Sarge.'

The rest of them turned around and took notice of the sergeant in the room with them.

Rakesh wished it was all respect for the rank, but he was mostly warning any constable with his back to the door that the boss was among them. He might be on the same team, but Rakesh was very definitely not one of them.

'Dean.' Rakesh returned the nod, then skirted around

the crowd and entered their toilet. Two doors were shut, blocking off the grunting, but the left-hand cubicle was empty. Four pristine rolls of toilet roll were stacked up above the cistern, with another mounted on the wall and halfway through. He grabbed the top one and walked back through, then tried to nudge past the group.

Bell stood up and blocked his path. His back was etched with a giant tattoo of a boxer holding up a belt, the mirror image covering his skin.

Rakesh pointed at him. 'Is that you, George?'

Bell swivelled around to glower at Rakesh. Just wearing tight white briefs. Despite being mid-forties, his torso was chiselled like a Greek statue. He gave Rakesh the up and down. 'Is what me?'

'Your tattoo.'

Bell pulled a hand behind to rub at it. 'What? Who gets a tattoo of themselves?'

Rakesh shrugged. 'You might.'

The gang of officers laughed.

Bell pursed his lips, looking around and waiting until they stopped. 'It's Ken Buchanan.' His voice was a harsh uppercut.

Rakesh tossed the toilet roll in the air and caught it. 'And who's he when he's at home?'

'Edinburgh's best ever boxer, man. Fighter of the year in 1971. Ranked above Ali and Frasier.'

'Still haven't heard of him.' Rakesh nodded at him. 'See

you for your shift, George.' He took his toilet roll back out into the corridor, hoping he'd put Bell in his place enough. He opened the door to the sergeants' room, then stepped in.

Sergeant Richard Marjoribanks was rummaging around in his locker, still dressed in his uniform. He looked around at Rakesh, then went back to it. Then stopped and turned around, frowning. 'Have you started bringing your own bog roll to work?'

Rakesh sat on the bench and toyed with the toilet paper. 'Someone used up the last roll and hadn't replenished it.' He threw it in the air again, but missed, and it rolled across the floor. He reached down and picked it up. 'Aren't you still on shift?'

'Aye. Supposed to be.' Marjoribanks clawed at his skull like something was squeezing it. 'Just had to come in to get some paracetamol. Day shift's been hell, mate. *Hell.*' He sat and popped a pill out of a blister pack. He stared at it instead of swallowing it. 'Bugger of a case. Fourteen-year-old lassie from Danderhall went missing. Still haven't found her.'

Rakesh leaned forward with his head in his hands. 'This going to have an effect on back shift?'

'Oh, aye. Big time.'

Rakesh slipped his T-shirt over his head. 'Fantastic.' He pulled his jeans down, then stowed it all away in his locker.

'You're hating this stint in uniform, aren't you?'

Rakesh stood there in his Y-fronts. Then hauled on his standard-issue trousers. 'Is it that obvious?'

'Blatant.'

Rakesh buttoned up his trousers. 'Can't believe it's only two months since my time in Professional Standards and Ethics ended.' He pulled on his polo shirt and it felt even tighter today. 'Feels like years ago.'

Marjoribanks finally popped the paracetamol into his mouth then glugged down some water. 'I don't understand why you're so desperate to go back to being a detective. Been there, done that, pal. Uniform life is way better. You just love 'em and leave 'em. Nobody bothering you on your days off. Nobody getting you up in the middle of the night. Nobody squawking about not paying you overtime when you come in. And if you want my opinion, a uniform sergeant is the best gig going. Money's good, you get a lot of respect and autonomy, but hardly any pressure.'

Rakesh sat back and processed it rather than hauling on those awful shoes. 'It just feels like I can make more of a difference as a detective.'

'That implies you don't think you're making a difference here?'

'Not in the same way.' Rakesh raised a finger. 'Don't tell Asher.'

Marjoribanks laughed as he finished his drink. 'Still got your iron in the fire down in Gala, though, right?'

'Supposedly. Trouble is, the metal's gone a bit cold.'

'Meaning your potential new boss hasn't got back to

you.' Marjoribanks got up and patted Rakesh on the arm. 'Plenty other fish in the sea, pal.'

'True, but my bait is all mouldy.'

Marjoribanks laughed, then left the room.

Rakesh sat forward and laced up his shoes. He was glad nobody could hear the sigh and comment on it. He grabbed the toilet roll then finally walked through for his pre-shift jobbie.

# CHAPTER TWO

Rakesh entered the squad room and those shoes were tucking a bit too tight. He should order a bigger pair, but really – he'd be gone soon and could choose his own sodding footwear.

He'd hoped the room would be empty and he could get on with his prep, but Inspector Hamish Asher was lurking by the whiteboard mounted on the far wall, pen uncapped in his giant farmer's hands. His Cro-Magnon forehead jutted out, hiding his shifty eyes. The whole look made it a surprise that he knew how to use a pen, and not just as a crude weapon. Somehow he'd got himself all sunburnt, despite it being November, his pale skin tinted a bright red, his thinning hair not exactly providing much of a barrier to the sun. He looked around at Rakesh and flashed a smile. 'Afternoon, Rakesh. How are you doing today?'

Rakesh joined him by the board. He'd never tire of the smell of whiteboard marker. 'Hard to get excited by back shift, sir. Five until three on a Saturday in November.'

'The worst one for sure. You've just slugged through the same routine on a Friday only to have a second verse, the same as the first, but one night later. Always remember, you've got this shift and then that's your rotation done.' Asher slapped his arm hard. 'Four days off, eh?'

'I've been dreaming of it for the whole rotation, sir.' Rakesh cast his gaze across the board and felt a bit sick. Still a few static cases that'd never shift and couldn't be palmed off to anyone, given they were the bottom of the barrel. But Asher's prehistoric handwriting had scrawled a new one in giant red letters:

MisPer: Dawn O'Keefe, 14, Danderhall

Rakesh tapped the name. 'Heard about that from Marjoribanks.'

'Nightmare.' Asher grimaced and it seemed like his forehead swelled up. 'It's been ten hours now. Lassie didn't show up at school yesterday. Mum didn't find out till later due to some stupid admin blunder. She went looking for her. Finally gave up and called it in this morning.'

'So, a day after she went missing?'

'Right. Talk about the trail going cold, eh?'

'Will you need—'

'Half of your team's been assigned, aye.'

The joy of being a uniform sergeant – your team wasn't your own, despite what everyone said. Despite what Marjoribanks believed. All the pressure of autonomy piled on your shoulders and they could snatch away half of your team with a moment's notice. On a Saturday night in Niddrie. And it was St Andrew's Day with its free whisky chasers with each pint.

'I need Hale and Taylor, sir. You can have Bell.'

Asher threw his head back and laughed. 'I know that game, Rakesh. Even wrote the rulebook on it. Invented all the tricks. So I know what you're doing – you pass me the arsehole and keep the good ones.' He gave a wry grin and held it for way longer than was comfortable. 'I just need four skulls, Rakesh. Don't care who.' He laughed. 'Actually, just not George bloody Bell.'

'Why's that, sir?'

'Skillset doesn't match. He's better at sorting out a swedge in a boozer than hunting for a lassie.' Asher yawned into his fist. 'I'll let you get on with your prep, Rakesh, while I track down a serviceable cup of coffee in this place.'

'Thank you, sir. Those cars won't assign themselves, will they?'

'Nope.' Asher walked off. Then stopped by the door. 'Actually, now you mention it... There's a bit of an issue with the cars because of Marjoribanks's team...'

## CHAPTER THREE

The small window at the back of the squad room showed the darkness spreading outside, sprinkled with a few yellow and white lights.

Rakesh stood at the front of the room, hands in pockets, even though the trousers were definitely a *lot* on the tight side. The only thing the lectern was good for was hiding that unseemly bulge from the team. Another thing he needed to order, or should if he was going to stay here longer than another month.

Seven cops sat facing him. Arms folded. Two banks of two desks, two per desk. One missing. And not for the first time this week.

Rakesh pointed at the four on the left. 'Upshot of all that is that Dean, Si, Ayesha and Carly will be supporting Sergeant Marjoribanks and his team in the hunt for Dawn

O'Keefe.' He held up a stack of papers. 'I've made printouts of her picture and details. Can you grab one on your way out?'

All four looked around each other, arms still folded, then faced the front again.

Rakesh cleared his throat. 'The request was for you to get on with it immediately.'

Chair legs scraped off the tatty lino.

'Sarge.'

'See you next week.'

'Have a good weekend, Sarge.'

'Be back before you know it.'

Rakesh watched the last of them shuffle out of the room. He was left with three officers. For an entire back shift.

*Spectacular...*

Bell sat up tall, looking a bit miffed by his exclusion from the task force, even if it was just going to be driving around southern Edinburgh for an evening until the wee sma' hours.

PC Ella Hale leaned forward, her skin a few shades darker than Rakesh's own, but she didn't say anything, just tightened her frizzy ponytail again.

PC Helen Taylor tossed a pencil in the air like a rock drummer would a drumstick and caught it with a twirling flourish. Her silvery-blonde hair was functionally short, nowhere near long enough to tie back.

The door flew open and PC Liam Inglis rushed in. 'Sorry, Sarge.' He slumped in the chair next to Ella, panting hard. 'Car wouldn't start.'

Rakesh stood up tall. Taylor and Bell were both older than him, which made exerting his authority that bit more important, especially for a repeat offender like Liam. And they both knew the games and moves, meaning he had to exert that authority over the younger members of the team and hope they respected that at least. 'You need to leave enough time for such things, Constable.' He checked his watch. 'This isn't the first time you've been late this week, is it?'

'No, Sarge. Sorry, Sarge. Need to trade in that shit heap.'

'That'd be a good move. Were you at the football?'

'What, no.'

'What was the score?'

'Hearts won 2-0.'

'But you weren't there?'

'No, Sarge. Had the radio on as I drove in.'

'That better be the truth.' Rakesh held his gaze long enough to hopefully let him get the message. 'Okay, so—'

'Where's everyone else?' Liam was looking around the room.

'They've been temporarily reassigned for this shift. Hopefully just the start, as I suspect things will get spicy later.'

Liam nodded like he understood everything. 'Sarge.'

Rakesh looked at the other three officers. 'Okay, so assignments are Ella and George, Liam and Helen.' He waited for four nods, but got a confusion of looks and glares.

Helen rolled her eyes.

Bell grunted.

At least Liam and Ella both nodded.

'Sadly, because Sergeant Marjoribanks's team are working overtime on this disappearance, they've still got the pick of the squad cars, meaning we've got the Volvo with the still-buggered clutch and the one with the faulty cage in the back.'

Bell raised a hand. 'Bagsy ECC17.'

Helen groaned. 'That's not bloody fair. That clutch is fu— gubbed.'

'You snooze, you lose, Hel.' Bell smirked. 'You of all people should know how it works.'

Helen sat back, shooting him a hard look. 'What's that supposed to mean?'

'Precisely what you think it does.'

'Okay, team.' Rakesh looked at Bell and Ella, the left-hand pair of desks. 'George, Ella, you're in 17. Piece break at nine, okay?'

Ella nodded. 'Cool.'

Bell scratched his neck. 'I'd prefer eleven, Sarge.'

'Of course you would. And I'd prefer to be a lottery

winner, but we're both disappointed.' Rakesh paused for laughter. He got it. Even Bell joined in. 'But we need everyone on deck for chucking-out time, especially as it's St Andrew's Day, as I'm sure you appreciate given your vast experience. So you two are at nine.' He looked at Helen and Liam. 'And you're at ten. And in ECC18.'

Helen nodded. 'Sarge.'

'I'm in ECC15.' Rakesh walked over to the whiteboard. 'Okay, so on to the actual work, then. Given their redeployment onto this MisPer, we've been assigned follow-ups from day shift.' He looked at Bell. 'George and Ella, can you pick up the domestic from last night? Start with calling in with that social worker about those two kids.'

Ella nodded. 'Sure thing, Sarge.'

'Helen and Liam, you're on response, okay?'

They both nodded.

Rakesh felt a slight inkling of control over the rabble. And the crappy situation he'd been landed in with having to manage a south Edinburgh Saturday night with half his team.

Helen scraped her chair back but didn't get up. 'Sarge, just wondering if... Seeing as how day shift are still out, are there enough tasers to go round?'

'Keen to let someone ride the lightning?'

'No, it's just—'

'It's fine. I checked. There are just about enough.' Rakesh looked around the room. 'And I need to remind you all of the training directive to test your body-worn video and tasers before heading out. "I didn't know it wasn't working" doesn't cut it as an excuse with me, okay? The log has to show you tested it.'

The nods came even slower than before.

'Okay, gang. Be safe out there...'

## CHAPTER FOUR

Rakesh swung his patrol car around the main roundabout in Craigmillar, then spotted the pub up the back street heading south.

> The Pit Heid
> Niddrie's favourite saloon

Favourite of two, the other just recovering from yet another enforced closure and change of ownership.

The area might have gone through a lot of regeneration in the last twenty-five years, rebranding from Niddrie and its notoriety, but gentrified was the last word you'd use to describe this pub. Geriatric was the first.

A huge white monolith, dating back much further than even the houses the current lot had replaced. Not quite grand, just *old* – it looked okay during the day, with its tasteful dark grey and blue chalk, but no amount of Farrow & Ball could cover over these settlement cracks.

Rakesh parked his patrol car behind another, then got out into the cold night and put on his cap. He wished he'd worn something more substantial than a standard-issue Police Scotland fleece, because that vicious wind cut right through it.

His analysis was interrupted by shouts coming from inside.

'Arsehole!'

'Wanker!'

'—here and say that, you wee scrotum!'

The pub's front door was shut, so he walked over to the back entrance on the side street, where tall planks of wood hid what he presumed was a smoking area. He opened the gate and stepped into the sodden beer garden. Six rows of picnic benches with umbrellas showing last year's fashionable lager that was likely just a relabelling of its equivalent five years ago.

A man stood by the back door, sucking on a cigarette and staring at his phone with a smirk on his face. He looked up at Rakesh and stopped smiling. 'Help you, mate?'

'Do you work here?'

'For my sins.' The smoker thumbed behind himself at the pub. 'Your pals are in there already.'

'And why aren't you?'

'Even if there are two squads of neds squaring off, it's still my fag break.'

Rakesh smiled at that attitude. 'Cheers.' He slipped past him, then entered the Pit Heid.

The main body of the pub was styled like a saloon in an old Western, even with an upstairs area looking down. Two sets of stairs led up, both blocked off by chunky ropes.

The decor was dated — someone had clearly spent a lot of money on the place in the nineties, but nothing since.

An oak bar occupied the far wall, but the space just had four pumps along its length. This year's fashionable lager, a perennial generic, a cider and the safety of Guinness.

Not that Rakesh drank — he'd just picked up the lingo from colleagues.

Helen and Liam stood in front of the bar, separating two gangs of angry drunks shouting the odds at each other rather than at the horse racing playing on two giant tellies on either side of the room.

Clearly two factions: old lags with bulky arms and prison tattoos on their necks; a larger number of young neds, their sportswear and hoodies puffing them up like hens — probably all skin and bone underneath.

All of them clutched half-filled glasses of beer.

Glasses which could cause no end of damage to faces and bare skin.

Rakesh barged through the crowd and used a chair to jump up onto a table near the bar. 'Okay! Listen up!'

The shouting stopped.

Bell and Ella walked in through the front door, elbowing their way to join Helen and Liam in the middle of the throng.

'Who needs a free ride to jail tonight?' Rakesh scanned the crowd, but he didn't recognise anyone in there. 'No? Then get back to your own sides of the pub!' He put his hands together as if praying, then slowly separated them.

Despite the amount of alcohol flowing through their bloodstreams, both factions of the crowd got it and, mercifully, complied.

Liam and Bell took charge, providing a barrier to split the group in the middle.

Helen and Ella walked away to guard a door each.

Now they were separated, the two groups seemed to start calming down. Seemed to – there was still a throb of menace in the room. Even the way they breathed was aggressive...

'I'm Sergeant Rakesh Siyal.' He hopped down onto the floor and turned to the barman. 'Are you in charge here?'

The barman was roughly the same age as the older half of the gangs. Grey rockabilly hair swept away from Buddy Holly glasses. His pot belly poked out of the bottom of an orange polo shirt that had seen better days. 'Own the place, so I guess so.'

'You *own* it? As in, you don't lease it from a brewery?'

The barman nodded. 'Aye, meant what I said.' He had the long roll of syllables Rakesh had heard when based down in the Borders. 'Guess that means this is all my fault, not a brewery's. Blame it on the old man. Sentimental old sod bought it in 1992 because *his* old man used to be a miner around here, when they actually worked the pit. Hence the name. Spent a bucketload on doing it up and he couldn't shift the bams, could he? Caused him no end of stress. Ended up killing him, just like it's going to kill me.'

Rakesh waved at the gangs. 'Did you call this in?'

The barman shook his head. 'That was Tobias.' He pointed at the guy Rakesh had spoken to outside, now slipping under the bar rather than raising the bar flap. 'Thought we needed help, didn't you?'

'We did.' Tobias waved at the simmering tensions between the two rival gangs. 'We still do.'

Rakesh leaned against the bar, like he was ordering a drink. 'Okay. How about you tell us what's happened here tonight?'

The barman shrugged. 'Nothing's happened. Yet.'

'Feels like it's going to, mind.' Tobias rolled his eyes at him. Up close, they looked similar enough it made Rakesh wonder if they were related. Probably father and son, but he didn't want to guess. 'St Andrew's Day's one of our biggest nights in the year, especially when it falls on a weekend. Big fireworks display around the corner, right? Hardly any time since Bonfire Night, either. Usual shite, too — expect loads of aggro at it, right? And, of course, they're all getting tanked up in here. And Dad's throwing beer down their throats like it's going out of fashion.'

'Because I've got good business sense.' The barman laughed. 'Less good for you lot when we kick them out at closing.'

'Trouble's been brewing all afternoon, since we had the Rangers game on at lunchtime.' Tobias twisted his lips as he pointed into the crowd of neds, his finger trained on a slight figure dressed like a rapper. 'That wee bastard there has been winding up that big bastard there about a big loss he's made on the horses.' He shifted his finger to indicate a lumbering monster — mid-forties, dressed in smart jeans with a short-sleeved shirt that showed off powerful biceps.

The wee bastard was in the middle of the group of young neds. He readjusted his baseball cap and scratched at the groin of his bling tracksuit. Young-looking with a thick moustache and soul patch combo. He laughed at something, then jabbed a finger in the air.

The big bastard was at the vanguard of the group of older guys, all looking hard and street smart. Looked like he'd been inside, judging by the amateur dragon tattoo climbing his neck. He gave the wee bastard a 'come on' gesture with his fingers, all chunked up with rings covering green-ink tattoos on his knuckles.

Rakesh focused on the barman again. 'Who stays? Who goes?'

The barman reached under the counter for a towel, then started drying Guinness glasses like there was no problem. 'The older gentlemen are regulars.'

Rakesh took that as an instruction. 'Okay, sir. We'll handle this.' He walked over to the neds. 'Gents, we need you to—'

The wee bastard jabbed a finger at the big bastard again. 'Keep losing money like that, Johnnie, and people will know you're a fuckin' loser!'

The big bastard roared with laughter, then fixed a vicious stare at his opposite number. 'Come here and say that, Keegan.'

The wee bastard – Keegan – stepped forward. 'Said, if you keep losing—'

'Heard you say that. Asking if you meant it or wanted to recant your words?'

'Fuck me.' The barman's eyes were almost out on stalks. 'How old are you, son?'

A kid standing next to Keegan gave a sarcastic shrug, but didn't speak. He seemed to hide away in his thick hoodie. He took a long drink of his lager and burped. His pale face looked young, way too young to be drinking crap lager in a crap pub. He had a massive plook on the end of his nose and an upper lip that hadn't met a razor yet.

Keegan rested his pint glass on the bar and looked at

him with derision. He might be skinny, but he was tall, at least six foot. 'Happy Meal's nineteen, you old bastard.'

'Aye, bullshit he is.' The barman jabbed a finger at Happy Meal. 'You're not getting back in here without ID. *Legit* ID, not some shite from the back of a packet of cornflakes.'

Rakesh stepped between them and rounded on Keegan, flanked by two neds on either side. 'Can I have a look at your ID, sir?'

A splash of spit landed on Johnnie's cheek.

Happy Meal was wiping his lip.

Johnnie charged over toward him.

Rakesh planted a hand on his chest, stopping him. 'We all know you can fight your own fights, but I'm asking you not to.' He reached over to hand him a set of napkins from the bar. 'You enjoy your beer, sir, and leave him to us.' He stared hard at Johnnie.

Johnnie got it, nodding slightly, then stepping back, mopping the spit away.

Rakesh raised an eyebrow to Bell, then leaned in. 'Keep him this side of the bar.'

'Sarge.'

Rakesh looked over to the younger crowd, just in time to see Keegan slipping out through the back exit.

Ella was swamped by the neds, but seemed to be holding off a few of them.

No sign of Happy Meal in the throng.

Rakesh tugged on Liam's sleeve. 'Come on, you.' He

jogged over to the back of the pub, then slipped around Ella's commotion and followed Happy Meal and Keegan through the back door. 'Come on, Ella.'

Rakesh stepped outside, flanked by Liam and Ella, but there was no sign of Keegan or Happy Meal. 'Spread out.'

Ella frowned at him. 'Isn't them leaving a good result?'

'Sure, but I want to make sure they don't return.' Rakesh led them up the street.

'Look at the fireworks!' Liam was behind them, staring up into the dark sky as an orange explosion burst out across the rooftops of Niddrie. 'Wow!'

'Here!'

Rakesh swivelled around towards the direction of the shout.

Keegan held a firework in his hand. Happy Meal had a lighter and touched the flame towards the rocket.

Bell broke out of the pub's beer garden.

Now Happy Meal held the rocket, pointing it towards them.

A purple blast shot off in their direction.

'Get down!' Rakesh covered his face as he dragged Ella over.

A second burst whizzed past them.

A Roman candle.

Happy Meal had a Roman candle.

Another volley fizzed over their heads, sparking in the air and filling it with the stench of burning.

Someone squealed behind them.

Rakesh swung around.

Liam lay on his front, screaming. The Roman candle was wedged into his trousers, burning away. 'Ah, you bastard!' He clawed at his trousers and hauled them down, but the fabric was on fire now. His scream deepened.

Keegan's eyes went wide. His mouth wider. 'Oh fuck!'

Bell raced over to Keegan, and his boxer's stance was too powerful for a ned whose fighting nous probably came from watching American wrestling. One punch and Keegan fell to the ground.

Rakesh looked around.

Ella was crouching next to Liam, who was screaming like he was on fire.

Rakesh pressed the button on his radio. 'Control, we urgently need an ambulance. Officer down. Also, can you send back-up from Portobello or St Leonards? Over.' He stood there, watching Bell tackling Keegan on the ground, resisting the urge to sigh.

'Receiving. Dispatching units from Porty. Over.'

'Sergeant.' Asher's voice, sounding stern and trying to project authority. 'Can you expand on the extent of the injuries? Over.'

Rakesh looked over at Liam. 'Rather not do it over the air, sir. PC Inglis has had a close encounter with a firework. Over.'

'A *firework*? Over.'

'A Roman candle, sir. Over.'

'How close? Sorry, forget it. Okay, Rakesh, I'll meet you at the infirmary. Over and out.'

Keegan cracked Bell in the face with a sharp elbow.

Bell went down clutching his nose.

Rakesh set off towards Keegan.

Keegan got in another hit with his left foot and pushed Bell over.

Rakesh raced towards him but the rest of the ned gang swarmed him.

He reached for his baton.

Someone tripped him and he tumbled over. He landed on his hands, his baton staving his right thumb.

He braced himself for the mother of all kickings.

It didn't come – heavy footsteps drummed the ground.

He looked over – the neds were all running away from the pub.

Rakesh got himself to his feet, then walked over to help Bell up. 'You okay there?'

Blood streamed from Bell's nose. 'I'b fibe, Sarge.' He rubbed it away. More blood poured out, dripping onto the pavement. 'Lucky shot, Sarge.'

'You're not fine.' Rakesh grabbed his arm. 'We need to get you and Liam to hospital.'

'Saib I'b fibe.' Bell rubbed his nose again. 'I'm fine.' No more blood. 'He got me with a lucky shot. That's all. I'm fine.'

'Okay, but *he's* not.' Rakesh pointed over to Liam.

'Fucking hell.' Bell walked over to Liam. 'You okay there, mate?'

The only answer he got was a fresh round of screams.

Ella looked back up. 'Ambulance is ten minutes away.'

Bell nodded. 'I'll stay with him.'

The beer garden door opened again and Johnnie lumbered out, his mates piling out behind him, fists clenched – at least their glassware was inside.

Johnnie looked around the area. 'Fuck happened here?'

Rakesh stared hard at him. 'They got away.'

Johnnie shook his head. 'Fucking useless, aren't you?'

'Do you know Keegan?'

'Fuck makes you think that?'

'You seem to have history.'

'Nope.'

'And what about Happy Meal?'

Johnnie gave a wistful sigh. 'Wee toe rag has just moved to the area. Seems intent on fitting in with that crew. Bunch of wee shites to a man. Him gobbing at me was his initiation. Having to prove himself. Lucky he didn't get his arm broken.'

'Sure about that?'

'Sure.' Johnnie snorted. 'Have to say, I was worse at his age. About the same size too.' He patted his belly with a wet slap. 'I thickened out, mind.'

'Come on. Do you know where Happy Meal or Keegan live?'

'Oh, aye, but I don't work for you lot, so you can take a running jump.' The code. Despite their beef, Johnnie would never rat on Keegan or Happy Meal. 'You want to nick him? Got nothing to do with me.'

'Understood, sir.' Rakesh put a hand on his back and pointed back at the beer garden. 'Now, go and finish your pint. He's getting nicked tonight.'

Johnnie laughed. 'Have to catch the wee sod first.' He stood there, rasping the stubble on his chin. But he did piss off inside the pub and took his mates with him.

Rakesh let out a deep breath, then took a look around the area.

Bell sat with Liam, dabbing at his nose.

Ella was talking into her radio.

Helen appeared, looking around. She frowned. Then squinted at something. Then started running away. 'Sarge!'

Rakesh jogged off in her wake, following her away from the pub and the main road.

Helen took a hard right and disappeared into a modern housing estate.

Rakesh tried to speed up but his tight shoes and even tighter trousers weren't exactly helping. And his stab-proof weighed a ton and rattled like a ladder falling down a staircase. He rounded the corner and caught sight of Helen chasing after a ned.

Helen backed her target into a parking bay outside a block of flats.

Rakesh sprinted to catch up with them.

Helen had him cornered behind a car. 'You're coming with me.'

'Eh? Fuck have I done?'

'You kicked a police officer.' Helen pulled out her taser and trained it on him. 'I'm asking you nicely.'

Happy Meal laughed. 'Or what? You going to shoot me with that thing, you bitch? Won't work on MEEEEEEEE—'

Spikes dug into his chest and left thigh above the knee, the long wire trailing back to Helen's taser.

The wee bastard went down like a sack of rice, but a sack of rice that was jerking wildly.

Rakesh held out a hand. 'Cuffs.'

Helen handed him hers.

'Thanks.' Rakesh walked past her towards the prone figure of Happy Meal, then cuffed him. He stood up and Helen stopped tasering him. 'Take this clown back to the station and book him. Bell has to live with a split nose, but do this one for assault causing bodily harm on Liam. See if he knows where Keegan is. And if that's his first or last name. Then file a report and send it on to the detectives in local CID to investigate assault causing bodily harm.'

Helen was busy replacing the cartridge on her taser. 'Sarge.'

'Thank you.' Rakesh walked past her, then took the turning back to the pub and the three patrol cars.

Bell was helping Liam into the back of one. Liam let out a scream like a teething baby.

Ella noticed Rakesh. 'Ambulance got diverted to an incident on George Street. Something about a man with a sword.'

Bell pointed at his car. 'I was going to—'

'I've got it.' Rakesh smiled at them. 'Here, I'll take Liam to hospital. You get back out on patrol.'

# CHAPTER FIVE

Rakesh stood in the hospital corridor with a good view of Liam's room. And he wished he hadn't.

The poor sod was writhing around on his bed, screaming and moaning. He stopped, staring right at Rakesh with sadness in his eyes. 'Sorry, Sarge.'

To a young PC like Liam, his sergeant was his god. Even when he was late. He was ashamed he'd let his side down – not to mention being worried he'd be fired for being an incompetent tit.

Poor bastard wasn't cut out for police work. Perhaps a firing would be a small mercy, considering the people out there on the street.

'Sergeant.'

Rakesh swung around to face Asher's caveman face.

Marjoribanks stood alongside him, dressed in his civvies now. He looked past Rakesh. 'How's he doing?'

Rakesh looked into the room, just as the nurse shut the door. He took a breath, then turned back to them. 'Nurse says he's probably suffered second-degree burns from the rocket. A Roman candle. The flame got stuck in his trousers and set fire to his pants. Burned the skin around his back door. Doc's having a look soon.' He grimaced. 'There might be some internal injuries too.'

'Fuck me.' Marjoribanks looked like he was going to be sick.

Asher screwed up his face and his eyes disappeared under that brow. 'Internal?'

'The blend of his trousers wasn't exactly non-flammable, so it—'

Asher raised a hand. 'I get it.' He shut his eyes now. 'But they're hopeful?'

'Don't know. It's clear he's going to be in overnight. The nurse thinks he could get home tomorrow, but...'

'But a doctor hasn't seen him?'

Rakesh nodded. 'That's right, sir.'

'Then it's going to be a long, hard road, isn't it?' Marjoribanks whistled. 'Listen, they've brought in a search coordinator, so I'm finally off duty now. Let me stay with him for a bit.'

'Thank you, Richard.' Asher raised his hands. 'But you're back on the clock until family show up, okay?'

'Are you sure, sir?'

Asher nodded. 'I look after my team. Keep me informed.'

'Sure.' Marjoribanks frowned. 'I'll call his mum and see if she wants a lift in.'

Rakesh frowned. 'You know her?'

Marjoribanks nodded. 'Liam worked for me back when I was a constable. I was his mentor.' He brushed at his cheek. 'You get close, don't you?'

Rakesh returned the nod. 'You do.' He clapped his arm. 'Thanks. Keep us updated.'

Marjoribanks winced. 'Will do, mate.' He walked over to the room and knocked on the door. 'How's it going, Liam? Heard you hurt your arse?'

Rakesh took a last look at Liam, now mercifully still, then caught Asher's glare, so he followed him through the hospital.

Asher walked with surprising grace, like he was sliding his way along the corridor. 'Poor kid. Have you got the wee toe rag who did this?'

Rakesh struggled to keep pace. Struggled to argue with the sentiment behind the term. 'Happy Meal.'

'Happy Meal? You don't have a name?'

'I brought Liam here, sir, but he's in custody. Meanwhile, George Bell managed to get an ID on the wee sod who elbowed him. He's still in the wind, but his name is Keegan Tait.'

'George won't settle for that.'

'He was the ringleader. Suggest we find him, charge him and see if it teaches him a lesson.'

'Okay.' Asher scowled. 'Thing is, there's a bit of a

manpower issue. Still haven't found that missing lassie yet, and I've had to send Richard's team home as they're already running on red in terms of OT. Half of Polly's team came in early to support the MIT with that sword thing in the centre and the other half are sucked up by this missing lassie. Dawn.' He looked around at Rakesh. 'Upshot is it's slim pickings out there for your mob.'

Rakesh felt the weight of being the only sergeant on shift in a quarter of Edinburgh. 'And now we're a man down now. Sir, I've only got three people working for me. And we've got to—'

'Relax, Sergeant.' Asher held the door for Rakesh. 'Tommy Braithwaite's being reassigned from Portobello. He's good. So until he turns up, I suggest you let Bell fly solo.'

'Bell?'

'Well, he's done that so many times.' Asher laughed. 'Probably even prefers it. Bit of a Judge Dredd power trip with that guy, but he's effective.'

'Is being on a power trip a good thing?'

'Not really, but it's a solid option, isn't it?'

'Guess so, sir.'

'And Ella and Helen could double up once Helen is done booking Short Stack.'

'Happy Meal.'

'Right.' Asher laughed. 'Happy Meal. That's a good one, have to say.'

Rakesh didn't appreciate any quality of nicknames so

kept quiet. He followed Asher out into the car park. Cold now, but the clear day had given way to a night thick with cloud cover, the city's lights casting the ominous gloom bright from below.

'I'll see you back at the station.' Asher got in his car, filling a disabled bay, then drove off.

Rakesh waited for a car to trundle around looking for a space, then walked across what felt like the entire car park to get to his vehicle. He got in behind the wheel and tried to get Liam's screams out of his head.

The kid clearly wasn't up to it, but nobody seemed to care.

Bottom line, that had happened on his watch.

To someone like Asher, Liam was a row on a spreadsheet. A bum on a seat, even if that bum was now scarred.

Injured like that in the line of duty...

Rakesh was learning the hard way that the problem with frontline policing was the expectation that you both gave and took a few bumps along the way.

He knew he should come in tomorrow with a magazine and a bottle of Lucozade. On his day off. That's what superior officers did, right?

He logged in to the car, but didn't start the engine and instead went into the group chat.

Nobody had posted anything. Hopefully they were all behind their wheels, driving around and doing whatever was needed to track down Keegan.

Rakesh started typing:

> Any joy getting on tracing Keegan Tait?

He sent it then sat back, staring at the hospital. He remembered when it was being built, how everyone talked about it around the city. And now it was part of the city's bedrock, really. Before he knew it, it'd be at risk of being replaced itself by something newer.

Then again, he'd been to the Western General recently and if anything needed to be replaced…

There was a long queue of public works, that was for sure, and nobody in the city council or Scottish government would commit to that spend again, not after the heat they'd got from the trams.

Rakesh checked the group chat again.

*George Bell is typing…*

But still not sending anything. Typical.

It stopped. Then started up again. Then the laptop chimed.

BELL:

> No sign of him, Sarge. I've just been called to a domestic. Until Tommy turns up, I'll need back-up.

Rakesh sighed – he shouldn't have to do this kind of thing, but he was finding out that what uniform sergeants did by default was supervise and fill in where needed…

# CHAPTER SIX

Lygon Road was one of those streets you drove past and didn't think about – unless you got diverted down it as a result of an accident, like Rakesh had once. It wasn't far from the Cameron Toll shopping centre and the King's Buildings campus of Edinburgh uni – Rakesh had friends who'd studied there, but had never visited. Neither were visible from here.

Rakesh pulled up outside a fancy semi-detached house, the kind you saw everywhere in old Edinburgh. Not the sort of place you expected a domestic, but then where was? He got out into thin rain that had started without warning, but couldn't see any signs of a disturbance.

Or of Bell's squad car.

Typical.

Headlights traced from the main road and, sure

enough, there it was – ECC17 in all its glory. Not that it was that different to the other two they had just now, but you got to know these cars inside out. Their buggered clutches and damaged cages. Ignitions you had to pulse to get going.

Bell parked behind Rakesh and got out too. He looked like a mess – fresh blood dribbled from his nose, which he wiped away. He gave Rakesh a nod and looked up at the house. 'Sarge.'

Rakesh let out a sigh. 'Forget Liam, *you* should be in hospital too.'

Bell rubbed at his nose again. 'I'm fine.'

'You don't look it.'

'Totally fine, Sarge. Been out looking for the wee sod who did this to me.' Bell patted his nose tentatively. 'Ah, you bugger.'

'It clearly isn't fine.'

'Right. Thought it, but *ow*!' Bell bared his teeth. 'I was on the verge of thinking of maybe heading to hospital when this call came in.' He pointed at the house. 'And here we are.'

Rakesh could press this, but this wasn't the time. So he put his cap on, like the coward he was. 'Neighbour called it in, right?'

'Aye.' Bell kept his cap in his hand. 'Drunk husband, apparently. Clearly threatening his wife. According to the caller.'

Rakesh checked the two main suspects – either the

neighbour who shared a wall with the address or the one on the other side of the drive. Maybe someone over the road, but probably either of those. Or both. 'Okay. Let's do this, then you're going to hospital.'

'Deal.' Bell started walking up the path. 'Hate these domestic calls, Sarge. You make an arrest, then they're back in love before the ink dries on the charge sheet and you're the villain. Not to mention clogging up the courts with a contested prosecution. "Don't run a trial. It's all my fault. I won't testify, he didn't mean it".' He slapped his cap on. 'You don't arrest them and you're called a lazy sod by all the lads in the station.'

Rakesh could've said those words himself. Even in his short stint in uniform, he'd seen way more than he'd expected of that kind of thing.

Bell walked up to the door and the Ring doorbell camera glowed blue even without him pressing the button.

Rakesh flipped down his video camera. 'BWV.'

'Sarge.' Bell did the same, then pressed the doorbell's button and it chimed through its sequence.

The door opened too quickly and a man stared out. Well-dressed, medium height, slight build. Mid-thirties, maybe, but completely bald. 'Evening, officers. What's up?'

Bell stepped forward and tilted his head to the side. 'Good evening, sir. We've had a report of a disturbance at this address.'

The man frowned. '*Here?*'

'Mind if I take your name, sir?'

'It's Lennon.' His gaze swept between the two cops. 'Lennon Blackwell.'

'Are you here alone, Mr Blackwell?'

'No, I'm...' Lennon thumbed behind himself. 'My wife's in the kitchen.'

Bell beamed wide. 'You won't mind if we have a wee word with her, will you?'

Lennon folded his arms. 'She's fine.'

'I see.' Bell snorted, then plastered on a really patronising smile. 'Thing is, the sooner we speak to her, the sooner we can get out of your hair and let you get on with your evening.'

Lennon considered it for a few seconds, then stepped aside. 'I guess so.'

'Thank you for your co-operation, sir.' Bell stepped into the house and stepped a bit too close to Lennon, like he was trying to physically intimidate him.

Rakesh had learned to use that trick himself. He hated that he had to, but a man who'd been threatening his wife didn't deserve respect. He followed Bell through a nice home with a tasteful paint job and lush carpet, into a kitchen that was a complete disaster zone. Clearly in the middle of being renovated, with a fancy oak table the only decent thing there. A buggered Aga spat away, stuffed between some plywood units direct from an eighties showroom.

A woman in her early thirties stood by the window, looking out across the back lawn. Didn't even so much as glance across at them.

Lennon sort of hovered in the space between them. 'Apologies for the mess. We're in the middle of renovating. This is my dad's old place, which I inherited and... It needs a lot of work, as you can see.' He gestured at the woman. 'Sorry. This is Phoebe. My wife. Babe, this is the police. They want to speak to you.'

She still wouldn't look at them, just kept her focus on the window. Maybe she was watching them in the dark glass, but Rakesh couldn't tell from her blurry reflection.

Bell moved into the space between them, then took off his cap and stepped closer to Phoebe. 'Hi there, Phoebe. You okay?'

She looked down at the floor now. 'I'm fine.'

'Sure about that?'

Lennon ran a hand across his bald head. He picked up a fancy iPad and snapped it shut, then set it down on the table. 'What's this about?'

Bell kept his focus on Phoebe, but she wasn't looking at him. 'Reason we're here, Phoebe, is we had reports of a disturbance. Raised voices.' He held up his hands. 'Don't get me wrong, we all raise our voices, don't we? I totally get it. Something happens, tempers get frayed, we end up shouting. But the last thing we all want is for this to escalate any further, right?'

Lennon took another step closer to them. 'There's nothing happening here.'

Bell was still focusing on Phoebe. 'You okay there, Mrs Blackwell?'

Phoebe looked up at Bell, then her eyes narrowed. She looked him up and down, then shot a glance at her husband, then back at Bell. 'No. I'm not okay.'

Bell gave her a polite smile. 'You want to tell us what's happened here?'

She looked away. 'The usual.'

'Sorry to hear that.' Bell left a pause. 'What does that mean, though?'

Phoebe swallowed, then looked at her husband. 'He was shouting at me.'

Bell nodded along with it. 'Is that all?'

'That's all.'

'He didn't hit you?'

'He'd never hit me.' Phoebe kept looking at Lennon. 'Right?'

Lennon was nodding furiously now. 'Of course not.'

'Okay, so this hasn't escalated, then.' Bell tilted his head to the side. He was good – and knew it. 'That's still not fine, though. What was he shouting at you, Phoebe?'

She rubbed at her eyes. 'Saying... saying he's going to...' Her voice cracked, like the glass from a thousand broken mirrors. She looked at Bell now. 'He said he's going to kill me.'

Bell stood up to his full height and towered over Lennon. 'Is that true, sir?'

Lennon laughed. 'This is fucking bullshit.'

Phoebe took a deep breath. 'He thinks I'm having an affair with someone.'

Lennon jabbed a finger in the air towards her. 'She fucking is!'

'Whoa, whoa.' Bell blocked him off. 'Let's keep this civil, shall we?'

'Civil? She's sucking someone else's cock in my own fucking house and I'm supposed to—'

'Calm down, sir, that's—'

'Lennon, you're mental! I'm not fucking any—'

'You're a fucking slut!'

Phoebe laughed at that. She arched an eyebrow as she folded her arms. 'Charming.'

Rakesh slipped between them, pressing his back against Bell's, facing Lennon while Bell faced her. 'Okay, so there's *clearly* something going on here. How about we—'

'Paranoid loser.' Now Phoebe was the one throwing imaginary fingers at her husband. 'You always think there's something going on. There fucking isn't. Never has been. If only you'd...'

Lennon's forehead pulsed and throbbed. 'If only I'd what?'

Phoebe looked away, shaking her head. 'Never mind.'

'No. Out with it! If only I'd what?'

Phoebe stared at him, like she was weighing something up. 'If only you'd fucking get over yourself.'

Lennon laughed, but there was no humour in it, only sheer malice. 'Get over myself?' He moved towards her. 'I'll fucking kill you!'

'That's it.' Bell launched himself forward. He grabbed Lennon by both arms and pushed him back against the wall. 'Okay, pal, you just stepped over the line.'

'What?'

Bell twisted him around so he was facing the wall now. 'We're taking you in, sir.'

'You're arresting me?'

Rakesh stepped to the side and grabbed Bell's cuffs off his belt, then applied them to Lennon's wrists while Bell held his arms. 'We tend to like to avoid locking people up, so we can—'

'Locking me up?' Lennon's angry gaze swivelled between them. 'What? You're taking the fucking piss here!'

'I'm serious, sir. This argument was loud enough for a neighbour to call it in. And now you've shouted at her and threatened her in the presence of me and my sergeant.' Bell pushed him, so his cheek pressed hard against the wall. 'Now, as nothing physical has happened, we could just settle this by separating you until you've calmed down. Let cooler heads prevail and all that, eh?' He paused to let the message sink in. 'But there's more than enough to charge you here, so I advise you to moderate your language and your actions.' He snapped the cuffs a little bit tight, another way of asserting dominance. 'Now, we're going to take you away, sir, and put you both in neutral corners. Then this will all be fine, okay?'

Lennon nodded. 'Fine.'

Bell turned him back around. 'Cool. You can discuss this matter together once you've had time to reflect on—'

'You stupid fucking bitch!'

Bell gave a withering look at Rakesh, then focused on Lennon. 'Lennon Blackwell, I am arresting you for a breach of the peace. You do not have to say anything—'

# CHAPTER SEVEN

Rakesh stood by the living room window, watching Bell cart Lennon out to the patrol car. The one with the dodgy cage separating the front and back. He had to hope it wouldn't be an issue.

Bell shoved him in the back, then stood there, breathing out. He caught Rakesh looking out at him and waved. He took a call on his radio, then turned away.

Rakesh still hadn't got word over Helen processing Happy Meal, so it was probably that.

He smiled, glad to see it wasn't just him who'd been saddled with a stupid nickname.

In a few minutes, Lennon Blackwell would be in processing in Craigmillar station. Then he'd be in a cell, sitting on hard concrete.

Hopefully he was already regretting his actions.

Hopefully he'd never even think of doing it again.

Rakesh let out a sigh – nobody could be *that* hopeful, not even his dad.

He certainly never could be.

Thing with what Lennon had done was once you'd crossed a line, it was impossible to go back.

Rakesh turned around and walked through to the kitchen, standing in the doorway.

Ella was sitting at the table, taking Phoebe's statement.

'Of course I'm not having an affair.' Phoebe gasped. 'Lennon's... He's just... He's the possessive type, right? Sees me as his object. He's so fragile he needs me to fuel his ego.' She nibbled at her bottom lip. 'Truth is, things haven't been great for ages.' She leaned forward to rest her elbows on the table. 'Work's been pretty tough for both of us. And...' Another gasp. 'We've been trying for a baby, but it's been two years... I know we're still young, but...'

Ella nodded. 'Took one of my colleagues a long time to have her first. A lot of trying. Then it happened. And the second came along not long after.'

Rakesh wondered if that was Helen she was talking about. They were friends, but that was a betrayal of trust. Wasn't it?

'I know it's stressful.' Ella leaned forward. 'I know the stress takes its toll on both of you. All the same, that's no excuse for anyone to act like that.'

Phoebe seemed to shrink away from her.

Ella rested her elbows on the table enough to flex her toned biceps. 'Stress isn't a reason to shout at someone. And *nothing* justifies threatening to kill someone, especially not your spouse.'

Phoebe looked over at the window, then locked eyes with Rakesh. She immediately looked away. 'No, but...'

Ella gave her a kind smile. 'How about you explain what happened?'

Phoebe sat back and folded her arms. Bad body language. Even her feet were coiled together, making her legs like two fighting snakes. 'Where do I start?'

'When did you get back from work?'

'About five. Busy day.'

'And where was he this evening?'

'At work. First dress rehearsal.'

'He's an actor?'

Phoebe shook her head. 'Lighting director.' She stared into space, as though on autopilot. 'He's really good at it but... Then they went out afterwards for a drink to discuss how it went. They open on Thursday. It's stressful, right? The director expects the lights and the music to do a lot of work to support the actors, but it can only do so much.'

'Are you involved?'

'Me? God, no. I run a lighting shop.'

Ella smiled. 'So you're both in the lighting game?'

'There's no lighting game.' Phoebe rolled her eyes. 'It's

my family business. Third generation now. Dad handed it over last year.'

'I'm sorry to hear that.'

'Oh no, he's still alive and well. He just decided to retire, out of the blue. And he did. Now him and Mum are away on a round-the-world cruise.' Phoebe clawed at her hair. 'Meanwhile, I'm left running the shop. And Jen isn't much help.'

'Jen?'

'Sorry. Jen's my sister. She tries her hardest, bless her, but... She's not got a business brain. Decent at selling, but...'

Ella left a long pause, but Phoebe didn't fill it. 'Okay, so what happened tonight when he got back?'

Phoebe shrugged. 'What's there to say? He came home and started having a go at me. Lennon's a really nice guy, you know?' She pinched her brow. 'Most of the time, anyway.'

'And when isn't he?'

'It's not that... It's... He just gets jealous. Especially when he's been drinking.'

'He didn't seem drunk.'

Phoebe shook her head, shaking her hair free. 'Even after one glass of wine. It's insane.' She let out a deep sigh. 'I don't want him charged.'

Ella sat back and folded her arms again. 'Why's that?'

'Because he loves me. And this whole thing is my fault.'

'What do you mean by that?'

'I mean... It is, isn't it?'

'Have you done anything?'

'No, but...'

'You said you haven't had an affair?'

'And I haven't been.'

'So I don't see how this can be your fault.'

Phoebe frowned hard. 'It's complicated.'

Ella reached out a hand and stroked her arm. 'We're here to listen, Phoebe.'

Phoebe took a halting breath. 'I know what he's like when he's been drinking. I should've just stayed out of his way instead of winding him up. I provoked him. Just like poking a stick into a wasp nest. Should know better by now.'

'It's very common in cases of domestic abuse for the vic—'

'Domestic *abuse*?'

'That's what this appears to be, Phoebe. He threatened to kill you.'

Phoebe stared at the floor again. 'Jesus...'

Ella looked over at Rakesh, then back to Phoebe. 'Okay, so we're taking Lennon to the station to give you both time and space to cool off. But mainly him. Once he's calm, we can evaluate the need for any charges.' She stood up. 'Meanwhile, we're going to take you somewhere else tonight, Phoebe. I can drop you at a friend's place?'

Phoebe looked up at her, a small child to their parent. 'Can't I stay here?'

Ella shook her head. 'That's not appropriate. If Lennon does get released, we need some assurances the whole thing isn't just going to start up again when he gets home.' She frowned. 'Where does your sister stay?'

Phoebe nibbled at a fingernail. 'Portobello.'

'Excellent.' Ella flashed a smile. 'Then I'll take you there, once you've grabbed a few things.'

Phoebe returned the nod. 'Okay.'

'That's that settled, then.' Ella caught Rakesh's stare and walked over to him, then dragged him out into the hallway. 'Can I get you a cuppa?'

'A cup of tea?'

'Aye, you look like you're getting comfortable on this call, Sarge. I could catch up with you later. Pretty sure you've other matters far more pressing. Like that missing girl?'

Rakesh looked her up and down, then smiled. 'Point taken.'

Ella was grinning wide. 'How much of that did you hear?'

'Enough.'

'Right. Well, she's not all that keen on charges. Do you want to let him go?'

'Not until he's sober.'

'He didn't seem pissed, Sarge.'

'No. But if he doesn't need alcohol to get violent, then

we have a problem if we let him go. George is taking him to the station now.' Rakesh waved out of the door. Except the patrol car was still there. 'Lennon can sit in a cell and think about what he's done. If he *is* drunk, then he won't be after a while. Once he's sobered up, we can get him to think through his actions.'

'I'll let you sort that out, then. See you later, Sarge.'

'Keep me updated.' Rakesh took a last look at Phoebe, still sitting in the kitchen, but she didn't seem to acknowledge his presence. He stepped over to the front door.

Just as Bell entered the house.

Rakesh frowned at him. 'I thought you were taking—'

Bell raised his hands. 'Relax, Sarge. Tommy Braithwaite's looking after him for me.'

'He turned up?'

'No, sir. He's using astral projection to babysit a suspect for me.' Bell laughed. 'Aye, he's outside. Got dropped off two minutes ago.' He scratched his neck. 'Wee problem, though. Tommy just got a call saying he needs to head back to base to be redeployed onto the hunt for this lassie.'

Rakesh couldn't help but let out a groan. 'You're kidding me?'

'What he told me.'

'Fine. I'll take it up with Inspector Asher.'

'Not my fight.' Bell pointed through to the kitchen. 'How's it going with her?'

'Just about done. Ella's going to take her to her sister's in Portobello.'

Bell patted his nose and seemed to recoil. 'I could do it on my way to the ERI?'

Rakesh scowled at him. 'It's not on the way, George.'

'It's not far, though. If you could drop Tommy and Lennon at the station, then it means you can put Helen and Ella onto finding this Keegan Tait, right?'

## CHAPTER EIGHT

Rakesh waited for the security gate to open, then watched it judder up to almost the full height, not that it ever got there.

Braithwaite was in the passenger seat, but it was like he was meditating. Just staring forward. What was it the kids called it, where they'd do nothing on a long-haul flight except stare straight ahead? Rawdogging or something. He was rawdogging this shift.

Rakesh trundled his patrol car through into the secure area behind Craigmillar station. All of the other cars were out, except for Asher's, so he had the pick of the spaces and slotted in right by the back door.

And Asher was the man he needed to have words with...

He got out and it was perishing, but at least the rain had stopped. The wind had picked up a lot, carrying a fug of second-hand cigarette smoke from somewhere Rakesh couldn't see.

Braithwaite got out and stuck his cap on. 'Sorry, Sarge.'

'Not your fault.' Rakesh flashed him a smile. 'Let me take it up with the boss.'

'Sure thing.' Braithwaite nodded, then walked off into the station.

Ella's car swept into the adjacent space.

Rakesh followed Braithwaite.

He held the door for someone.

Helen, walking over and giving Rakesh the nod. 'Where's Tommy off to?'

'Called onto the other case.'

'Why him and not us?'

'Because...' Rakesh didn't know. He plastered on a smile. 'Because I've got my core team.'

'Shame. Could've done with a bit of glamour for once.'

'I thought you were married?'

'Eh?'

'Tommy isn't exactly glamorous.'

'No, me getting a glamour case.'

'Right. With you now. Believe me, working on glamorous cases isn't all it's cracked up to be.' Rakesh smiled. 'Has Happy Meal been processed?'

'Gabriel McInvar, from Inverness. I swear, when I was wee, all you had were Davids, Andrews and the occasional

James. Now, it's like everyone's got to have a unique name.'

'Like Rakesh?'

'You know what I mean, Sarge.'

'So he's from Inverness?'

'Apparently. Says he's been staying here a few months.'

'He looks young. Too young to be living on his own.'

'Says he's eighteen.'

'And I could say I'm from Mars, but it doesn't make it true.'

Helen frowned at him, like she didn't quite seem to get what he was saying.

Ella got out of her car and opened the back door. 'Come on, you.'

Lennon seemed to be playing ball – he just planted his feet on the damp tarmac. He even let her walk him inside the station like a dog on a lead.

Rakesh followed Helen in after them.

'I hate domestic calls, Sarge.'

Rakesh sighed. 'I like to think of them as homicide preventions.'

Helen laughed. 'I like that. Never thought of it that way.'

'What is it you hate about them?'

'Just hate the time it takes, you know? Especially when we're this short...' Helen held the door for him.

The processing area was the worst part of an awful

station. The twin feelings of despair and regret seemed to seep into the exposed brickwork. That lack of care in the decor was reflected in the staffing.

PC James Wilson was tonight's shift security officer. Late forties and coasting to retirement. He whistled as he pressed the button, then the green light came on, indicating the mounted camera and microphone were operational. 'All ready for you, Hel.'

Helen led Lennon up to the counter. 'Sir, there's a video camera here to record the whole procedure.'

Lennon nodded at it, then swept his gaze around the room. Seemed to shiver, like the whole thing was finally hitting him. He swallowed and stared at Rakesh. 'Do I need a lawyer?'

'If you request one, sir, we'll certainly make the call.' Rakesh held that steely gaze. Those eyes were on the cusp of blue and green – hard to pin it down to one or the other. 'We don't dispense legal advice to decide whether you need one or not. That part's up to you.'

'You're arresting me. That's something. Isn't it?'

'A breach of the peace is a fairly minor charge, sir. We never want to deal with them, but when someone screams about wanting to kill their other half, it doesn't give us much of a choice but to act.'

Lennon rubbed at his temples. 'I'm a good man.'

Wilson barked out a laugh. 'They all say that.'

Lennon shot him a glare. 'I mean it. I work as a lighting tech at a theatre. That's an honest job, isn't it?'

'How did you get into that?'

'Lighting?' Lennon puffed out his cheeks. 'I just always wanted to do it. Been doing it since school. Not done any formal training, just... started doing it, you know? And never stopped. Learned on the job. At school, you know how you do plays and that? Guess they do that everywhere. Was never much of an actor, but at mine they let us do sound and lights too. You know, the kids who couldn't act for toffee. And I loved it. It's... It's like music, right? What I do adds to the magic of the show. You're emphasising stuff, masking the transition between the stages. Making people believe they're somewhere else. Medieval Edinburgh. Ancient Egypt. Broadway. The Scottish Parliament. Lighting goes a long way towards that.'

Rakesh nodded along with it. 'Big fan of the theatre myself.'

Lennon eyed him suspiciously. 'Aye?'

'Saw David Tennant as Hamlet down in London.'

Lennon raised his eyebrows. 'I'm impressed.'

'What are you working on now?'

'Just putting the final stages of the Christmas play together.' Lennon raised a finger. 'Not a panto, before you start. We're doing *Macbeth*, but it's set in the Scottish Parliament around the time of the independence referendum. Had to design all this crazy stuff that makes the audience think they're actually in the Parliament. I mean a lot of that's down to the production design, but how you light it is crucial.' He looked at Wilson, then at Rakesh. 'Surely you can see I'm a *good* man?'

Rakesh nodded like he was agreeing with him.

Lennon looked over at Wilson. 'Are you seriously going to charge me?'

'You can charm Sergeant Siyal about the theatre, sir, but that won't get you off anything.'

'I'm serious. I haven't done anything.'

Wilson snorted. 'Know what they say? Can't do the time, don't do the crime.'

Lennon stared at his feet. 'Come on, mate. She *made* me do it.'

The corners of Wilson's mouth turned up. 'Never heard that before...'

Rakesh shot Wilson a warning glance, then focused on Lennon. 'She made you threaten her?'

Lennon looked back up. 'Aye. When you were there, she was all sweetness and light. Just sat there, acting all calm and innocent, but... She didn't show her full self to you.'

*Full self...*

*Spoken like a wellness guru...*

'She's passive aggressive. *Very* passive aggressive.'

'In what way?'

'*Every* way, man. Every single way. Just constantly undermines me. All these wee barbed comments all the time. She snipes at me. Makes these cheeky asides. Constantly chipping away at my confidence.'

'Is that what she was doing tonight?'

'A bit.' Lennon sniffed. He rested against the counter, then stared into space. 'When I got back home, she was making dinner. She's a great cook. And I was starving.'

'Where had you been?'

'Working. I'd been in the pub with some mates.' Lennon swallowed. 'I say mates, but they're the director and some of the actors. The sound guy's a wanker, but you have to work with who you work with, right?' He shifted his gaze between Rakesh and Wilson. 'Sure you get that here. Anyway, Pheeb's sort of used to that world. She used to act, but her old man forced that business on her and she had to give it up. I mean, managing a shop like that at her age is a big undertaking. Takes up all of her time. And a lot of that is trying to unpick the stuff the old man did that didn't work and try new stuff that just might. And Jen's as useful as a chocolate lightbulb. Not sure how much money there'll be in it, but more than acting, that's for sure.' He cleared his throat. 'Anyway, today was our first dress rehearsal and things got a bit heated, so we agreed to blow off some steam in the pub. Chat over the problems over a drink or two. See what we can do tomorrow to make tomorrow's rehearsal go better.'

'Okay. That's all very interesting, but I fail to see how—'

'Because I heard from one of the lads that Pheeb's...' Lennon swallowed hard. 'That she's having an affair.'

That felt like the truth. Or at least Lennon's form of it.

Whether she was sleeping with someone else was another matter – it was crucial that he thought she was.

Rakesh left a long space for Lennon to add any further detail. 'That must've been a shock.'

'Tell me about it.'

'Did your source have—'

'The director. Jake.'

'Okay. Did Jake have anything to back it up?'

'What do you mean?'

'He said Phoebe had been having an affair. What was his evidence? Had he seen her with someone?'

'No.'

Rakesh scowled at him. 'So how did he know she was having an affair, then?'

'Because...' Lennon stroked his chin. 'Thing is, I was confiding in him, right? Telling him about how the... You know those Ring doorbell cameras?'

Rakesh nodded. 'I saw you have one, sir.'

'Right, of course. Well, the thing is, you're supposed to be able to answer the door wherever you are, right? Just pops up on your phone. I mean, if I'm in the middle of a production and there's a delivery, I can answer it. Simple.'

Rakesh frowned. 'Shouldn't you be working?'

'Should be. And during a performance, I am. My phone's in my locker, even. But during rehearsals, there's tons of time where Jake and the actors are, like, arguing and getting deep into stuff. "What's my motivation here?" All that nonsense. Occasionally they need a bit of joinery because some of the scenery isn't quite working. It's very rarely me or the arsehole behind the sound desk holding stuff up, so there's a lot of downtime for us.' Lennon shook his head. 'Anyway, I noticed the doorbell kept switching off when I was at work.' He flared his nostrils wide. 'And now I know why.'

Rakesh raised a hand. 'Hang on, you said your friend *knew* she was having an affair?'

'No.'

Rakesh looked at Wilson but saw his confusion mirrored. 'I'm not following. How did—'

'Jake *suggested* she was sleeping with someone else. Happened to him a few years ago. His ex-boyfriend was doing stuff behind his back. The Ring doorbell would go down for an hour every lunchtime. And these things shouldn't, right? You can wire them in, but I haven't done with ours and the battery on that lasts weeks. Or it should. But it kept being offline. Anyway. One day, Jake went home and caught his boyfriend at it with a delivery driver.'

'Was that what you were planning on doing today? Catching her with someone?'

'No. The doorbell was on the whole time.'

'So you were just going to confront her?'

'I did. I just... Asked her outright.'

'What did she say?'

'What do you think?' Lennon snarled. 'She denied it. Said I'm imagining things. But I listed all the times the doorbell had been all funny and she didn't have an answer for any of it. Refused to even engage me on the subject.'

Rakesh got out his notebook. 'When was it switched off?'

Lennon frowned. 'Half four every day.'

'Every single day?'

'Most days, anyway. Jen would take over the shop from four, so that was the time she'd get home.'

'And you weren't at home?'

'No. I was in the theatre then. Phoebe's shop's not far from home.'

Rakesh still felt it was all built on very shaky foundations. 'And you honestly think she was sleeping with someone?'

'Wouldn't *you* think that?'

'I'd get other evidence before I confronted her.'

'Such as?'

'Speak to a neighbour. If she was bringing men back there—'

'*Men?*'

Rakesh frowned. 'You think she was sleeping with a woman?'

'No, just... plural. Jesus, if she was shagging hundreds of guys behind my back... *Jesus.*'

'One or many, sir, surely she would've been seen by someone.'

Lennon looked up at the ceiling. 'Right.'

'Do you have any other evidence?'

Lennon shut his eyes. The sign of a man who'd seen red, exploded, then deeply regretted his actions. 'Not really, no.' He looked back down and stared at Rakesh. 'Look. I'm sorry. I shouldn't have done what I did.'

'And what was that, sir?'

'Shouldn't have shouted at her. Threatened to kill her. I just... She was winding me up. Really goading me. Grinding my gears. Maybe I am imagining things. Maybe there is a fault with the doorbell camera, you know? But I'm really, really sorry for what I said to her. I love her and I don't know what I'd do without her.' Lennon gave Rakesh a real puppy-dog look. 'Please, can I just go back home?'

Rakesh stood up to his full height. He was a few inches taller than Lennon and bulkier, but he didn't seem to intimidate him any. 'Let me think it over.'

'What's there to think about?'

'I need to review your record and check to see if we have any previous reports on you.'

'Thank you. I can assure you I have a clean slate.' Lennon reached out and grabbed Rakesh by the arm. 'I'm so sorry for all this.'

Rakesh looked down at his sleeve. 'Sir, I need you to let go.'

Lennon complied. Then seemed to crumble. 'I'm so fucking sorry. Please. I'll just go to my brother's. Won't speak to Pheeb. I swear. Then we'll meet somewhere neutral and in public and talk it all through.' He raised his hands. 'Please, I'm sorry. Really, really fucking sorry. I've made a mistake. I just want to get away. Put my head down. Then apologise to my wife. Please. Just let me go and I won't do it again.'

Wilson laughed. 'Aye, heard that before too.'

Rakesh shot a look at Wilson, then gave Lennon a firm glare. 'You're going to sit here and be a good boy while I decide whether to charge you or not.'

A furious glower passed across Lennon's face, then it seemed to simmer for a bit, then cool into a curt nod. 'Okay. Sure. Thank you.'

Rakesh walked him over to a set of seats at the side of the room, the fake blue leather was scratched and torn. 'Just wait here. PC Wilson will process you shortly.'

Lennon looked up at him with something like hope in his eyes. 'Sure. Of course.'

'Thank you.' Rakesh walked back over to Wilson and leaned on the counter. 'Was that recording?'

'Got it all down, aye.' Wilson laughed. 'Stupid prick admitted to threatening to kill his wife. I mean, on top of the body-worn video showing him actually doing it... Talk about open and shut, eh? What are you going to do?'

'I don't know.' Rakesh didn't like the power the constable wielded. The man's future probably rested on his decision.

Then again, like Wilson said – can't do the time, don't do the crime.

# CHAPTER NINE

Rakesh walked into the squad room and wished he hadn't.

Helen and Ella were over by the fridge, muttering under their breaths. Probably about him, their dickhead boss. Arsehole sergeant.

He'd heard them all and he wished the names just bounced off him. But they didn't.

Helen spotted him first and broke off from their chat. 'Just fetching our pieces from the fridge, Sarge.'

'Good idea. Means you can eat on the road.' Rakesh joined them. 'What have you got?'

Ella had a healthy salad in a clear plastic tub. Sprouts of lettuce and kale, plus more grated carrot than was surely good for you.

Helen had a kid's lunchbox emblazoned with Mario

riding a Yoshi. She opened it and the thing was stuffed with sandwiches.

'Looks good.' Rakesh crouched to get his own out, but some bugger had shoved two giant beakers full of protein shakes in front – probably Bell. That was all he ate. Rakesh wedged them in the door, where they belonged, then fetched his box. 'BWV uploaded?'

'Aye.'

Rakesh stood up and focused on Helen. 'And the form for CID?'

Helen sighed. 'I'll get on with it.'

'Remember the Use of Force form too.'

'For the taser?'

Rakesh could've been snide and joked about the cudgel made of fizzy strawberry laces, but he just nodded.

Helen smirked. 'Already in your inbox, Sarge.'

Rakesh frowned. 'Seems a bit quick.'

Helen shrugged. 'Not my first time using a taser, Sarge. Been doing this a long time. I was one of the first STOs.'

'Specially Trained Officers.' Rakesh grimaced. 'I hate abbreviations like that. As you know, I was a lawyer in a previous life. That whole industry is full of them.'

Ella was looking at him like he'd grown a third head. 'Don't see why it's bad, Sarge.'

'It sows confusion and it's elitist – it excludes people.'

'I can see that.' Ella raised an eyebrow. 'What made you become a cop, Sarge?'

'I forget most days.' Rakesh smiled at her, then looked at Helen. 'Anyway. I expected you to do it at the start of the next shift.'

'Why wait? The form's just a copy and paste job. Change a few details and bingo.'

'You shouldn't tell me that because I'll expect it even quicker next time. Assuming there's a next time.'

'With a taser?' Helen laughed as she made a fake pistol with her fingers. 'Oh, there's always a next time.'

'How many times have you—'

'Sixth time I've fired one this year.'

'This *year*? Bloody hell.'

'Don't call me Annie Oakley for nothing, Sarge.'

'Who's she?'

'Seriously?' Helen's eyes widened. 'One of the most famous cowgirls in the Wild West. Guess it was her or Calamity Jane and I'd fight anyone who called me that.'

'With good reason.' Rakesh smiled, but he did worry about her propensity to make people ride the lightning. 'Is Phoebe Blackwell at her sister's?'

Ella frowned. 'Bell took her, Sarge. Remember?'

Rakesh winced. 'Right. Of course. And her state—'

'Statement's in your inbox.'

'Excellent. Did you get anything new after I left?'

'Not really.'

Rakesh held Helen's gaze for a bit longer than strictly necessary. 'Does that mean you found something?'

'No. We've got nothing.' Ella glanced over at Helen,

like she was worried she'd let something slip. 'Phoebe said this is a one-off. Never been violent or abusive. And I checked. There's nothing on file for either one and no history at the address.'

'But they haven't lived there long, have they?'

'Eighteen months. Checked their previous address in Musselburgh and there's nothing there either.'

Helen took over. 'What are you going to do with him?'

'Lennon?'

'Aye. Wilson said you haven't charged him yet. Are you going to?'

Rakesh blew air up his face. 'I haven't decided yet.'

Ella tugged at her ponytail. 'We thought you should let him go.'

Rakesh rested his open-topped sandwich box on the table. 'That'd be my take on it too.'

Helen looked at his lunch then did a double take. 'What the hell have you got in there?'

Rakesh frowned. 'Sandwiches.'

'Is that...' She inched closer. 'Is that *egg*?'

Rakesh shrugged at her. 'Omelette sandwiches.'

'Omelette sandwiches? That's not a thing.'

'It is. You cook two small two-egg omelettes, then you put them between slices of buttered bread. Omelette sandwiches.'

Helen laughed. 'Seen it all now.' She pushed her box away. 'I've got haggis slice sandwiches because *he* thought it'd be funny to do that on St Andrew's Day.'

Rakesh frowned. 'Don't you like haggis?'

'Love it. Usually. When it's hot. But it's cold and greasy now.'

Someone knocked on the door.

Rakesh looked over.

Asher stood there, looking like he was wanting company on a quest for fire or needed help painting his cave walls. 'You got a minute, Sergeant?'

# CHAPTER TEN

Rakesh carried his sandwich box into Asher's office, then shut the door behind him.

Asher sat behind his desk and gestured at the seat. 'Please.'

Rakesh did as he was told, then set the box on the desk, but was now wary of revealing its contents in case he earned a second nickname. 'We were discussing the domestic, sir.'

'I got that.' Asher frowned at it. 'What have you got there?'

Rakesh pulled the box away and rested it on his knees. 'Just a sandwich.'

'Right. Starving myself.' Asher yawned into his fist. 'Been a hell of a shift already.'

Rakesh sat back and drummed his thumbs on the lid. 'Got a matter we need to discuss.'

Asher frowned at him. 'Go on?'

'I lost Braithwaite to the hunt for Dawn O'Keefe.'

'Ah.' Asher rubbed his thick forehead. 'Sorry, Rakesh. I should've told you directly.'

'That's right. I'm short a head and he was supposed to be it to make up numbers to half. And I only found out because he told me.'

'I know. Like I said, you shouldn't have found out that way. I'm trying to put it right, okay? I've put a call in to the boss to see if we can bring in some actual detectives and a proper search team, rather than depleting frontline resources.'

'So it's looking bad for her?'

'Teenagers missing this long are never good, are they?' Asher picked up his pen from his desk then immediately dropped it. 'Makes me think she's fled to the bright lights of London. Or the murky ones of Glasgow. Or she's buried in a ditch somewhere.' He looked at a photograph of Dawn O'Keefe, then cleared his throat and folded it in half, setting it aside. 'Anyway. Rich Marjoribanks just called to say he's left hospital. Said Liam's out of surgery and he's just going to fetch his mum.'

'How's Liam?'

'Not great. He's burned his arse cheek so it looks like a gammon steak.' Asher stifled a laugh. 'Won't be getting out tonight. Be back in surgery tomorrow to see if they can repair it.' He covered his mouth. 'Sorry, I shouldn't laugh... You were there, weren't you?'

'I was, sir.'

'And?'

'And what?'

Asher flung his hands out. 'Was it at least funny?'

'Funny?' Rakesh scowled at him. 'It was horrible. Happy Meal fired rockets at us. Liam hadn't noticed them and was facing the wrong way. A freak occurrence, but an incredibly painful one.'

'Happy Meal?'

'Full name is Gabriel McInvar.'

'I see.' Asher nodded slowly, with a grave look on his face. 'I take it your BWV was working?'

Rakesh narrowed his eyes. 'It's all uploaded, sir.'

'I should check it, then.' Asher cracked his knuckles, then worked away on his computer like a caveman trying to fashion some stone tools.

Rakesh stared at his sandwiches. His stomach rumbled. He didn't think he should eat but he was so hungry.

Voices burst out of the laptop's speakers, unclear and indistinct, but full of menace and threat.

Asher winced like he was watching a horror film. He covered his eyes. 'Oh no... His pants caught fire!' He burst out laughing. 'His poor *arse*!' He covered his eyes again. 'Oh God. Christ. I thought it was just the cheek, but no, that's gone *right* up his hoop. Christ on the cross.'

Rakesh sat back and folded his arms. 'I'm thinking we might release Lennon Blackwell.'

Asher looked over at him. 'Lennon who?'

'The domestic.'

Asher was still watching the video. He laughed again. 'Talk to me about it. What have you got? What have we done with him?'

'Neighbour reported it. He shouted death threats at his wife. We turned up, spoke to them and he threatened to kill her. It's on our BWV.' *But is clearly a lot less entertaining than watching a fellow officer get badly injure*d... 'Backed it up with a confession on the camera system at the processing desk.'

Asher winced again. 'And what do you want to do?'

'I'm debating releasing him versus a domestic violence charge.'

'But you haven't charged him yet, no?'

'Currently.'

Asher was clicking with his mouse. 'So let him go, then. No sense clogging the courts with something that doesn't belong there. '

Rakesh paused for a few seconds. The room was filled with Liam's screams. 'That's what Bell said.'

Asher looked over. 'Christ, I'm giving the same advice as George Bell?'

Rakesh nodded. 'He's got an opinion.'

'Know what they say. Opinions are like arseholes. Everyone's got one and they all stink.' Asher went back to watching the video. He grinned wide. 'Not all arseholes get burned like this, mind.' He leaned back, hands clasped behind his head. 'You think we should let this lad go?'

'Wonder if it's the better solution here. His wife didn't want to press charges. Blamed herself.'

Asher winced. For once it wasn't at the video footage. 'Red flag for domestic abuse, that.'

'I know. But it could also be the truth.'

Asher looked over at him, eyebrows raised. 'Jesus, are you serious?'

Rakesh shrugged. 'I'm just saying, if she's the antagonist, then maybe it *is* her fault.'

'Rakesh, for God's sake!'

'Come on, sir. We don't have evidence of what happened when we weren't there. I want to keep them apart and build a case.'

'Whatever ideas you've got about this job, Rakesh, it's not about building cases.' Asher focused hard on him. 'You're a uniformed officer now, not a detective. We've got so much nonsense to get through in the average shift, we don't have time to bloody eat, let alone build a sodding case.'

'Point taken.'

'But...' Asher sighed. 'All the same, it might be worth letting him stew a bit longer.'

'How about investigative liberation?'

'O-kay.' Asher sat forward and rubbed his fingers together. 'What do you propose?'

'No charge now, but he has to follow conditions for up

to twenty-eight days. Say he's not allowed to go to their home or communicate with his wife without a third party being present. Meanwhile, we continue our investigation, with support from the local CID, then we report to the fiscal.'

'Remember what I said about you not being a detective anymore?' Asher gave him a stern look, his jutting forebrow making it look even harsher. 'It's a lot of work. And our workload is crazy just now. And we'll be down a skull with Liam's arse.' He laughed. 'Bottom line.' He sucked in a sharp breath. 'Sorry, another inadvertent pun there. Effectively, I want it to be your decision, Rakesh.'

'Thank you, sir.'

'When you were in the Complaints, it was all about what the super wanted. But out here in the real world, you're a sergeant and *you* make the decisions. Not me. Not my boss. Not a super. You. Okay?' Asher got up and walked past, brushing Rakesh's shoulder as he passed. 'I'll leave it up to you.'

Rakesh sat there as the door shut, fiddling with the clasps on his sandwich box. 'Thank *you*, sir.' He clipped it shut, then got up and stomped over to the door.

# CHAPTER ELEVEN

Rakesh walked back into the processing area, trying to stroll like he owned the place. No sign of Wilson, for once, so he walked through into the cells.

Lennon was sitting on his concrete sofa, head in hands. He seemed in a worse condition than what he was sitting on. He looked up at Rakesh, with the hope in his eyes of a man in A&E waiting to be seen after four hours while his nose bled onto the floor.

Rakesh stopped in the doorway, hands on his hips, waiting for Lennon to look up, but he didn't. 'Mr Blackwell?'

Lennon locked eyes with him through the bars. 'What?'

Rakesh opened the cell and stepped aside. 'Come on.'

'You're letting me go?'

'After a fashion, yes.'

'Thank God.' Lennon got up in a hurry and followed him through to the desk. He didn't say anything, but his eyes were a vivid mixture of fear and hope. Fear over what he might be charged with, hope at getting off with it – his particular blend seemed to sit much more on the side of fear.

Rakesh rested a sheet of paper on the desk. 'Mr Blackwell, I need you to sign this and to agree to abide by the conditions stated there. Once you've signed, if you fail to follow them we can and will arrest you for breaching your undertaking.' He slid the paper across for Lennon to read.

Hunger filled Lennon's eyes as he skimmed. The desire to be free and out in the world, without a criminal record. He reached for the pen.

'I suggest you take your time reading that.'

'Of course.' His lips twitched as he read every word. 'So I'm not to speak to Phoebe?'

'That's correct. My team will follow up with you both in two weeks. In that time, you're not to speak to your wife without a third party present. And you're not to visit your home address.' Rakesh handed him a page. 'Will you abide by these conditions?'

Lennon took the pen but didn't sign it. 'Feels like I don't have much of a choice here.' He pressed the nib onto the paper, then pulled it away again. He looked over at Rakesh. 'Did Phoebe ask for this?'

'She's not party to this decision, no.'

'Do I have a choice here?'

'You can sign it. If you refuse to agree to the terms specified, you'll be held in custody pending charges. Your call.'

Lennon shook his head slowly, then stared at the pen. 'Fuck it.' He signed the page and handed it back. 'I'll go to my brother's, then.' He ran a hand down his face. 'But I need to get some stuff from home first.'

Rakesh knew this sort of wheedling would happen. 'Your wife isn't currently there, but we can arrange for someone to collect some of your possession upon her return.'

'I can't just pop in?'

'No. You've just signed an agreement to that effect.'

Lennon took the page and read it carefully, like there was a mistake he could pick Rakesh up on. He seemed to deflate. 'Mind giving me a lift to Dylan's?'

Rakesh almost laughed at the cheek. He'd bent over backwards for this guy and he was just going to keep pushing, wasn't he? 'I haven't got the time, I'm afraid. Call your brother or a friend. You could get a taxi or you could get the bus there. Or you could ride Shank's pony.'

Lennon stared at his feet. 'I'll get a taxi. Brother's a cabbie.'

Rakesh held his gaze. 'This is the last time I want to see you, okay?'

'Don't need to tell me twice. Thank you.' Lennon

walked through the door, then across the reception area, where a couple were sitting, facing away from each other.

Probably another domestic like him and Phoebe. At least they didn't have to be forcibly separated.

Lennon stopped outside the front door and tugged up his collar against the rain. He got out his phone and called someone. 'Hi.' He paused. 'Aye.' Another pause. 'Aye… She's talking to the bloody cops.' A further pause. 'I know! See you there.'

Rakesh was about to follow him through to give him another warning, but a taxi turned up and a lawyer got out, his suit simultaneously too big and too tight.

Lennon flagged down the cab and hopped in the back.

The lawyer waddled into the station, swinging his briefcase like a primary school child would. 'Evening, Rakesh.' He looked at his uniform. 'Bit late for Hallowe'en!'

Rakesh smiled now he finally recognised him. 'Long story, Pete. Long story.'

'Be glad to hear all about it.' The lawyer walked over to the reception desk and pressed the buzzer, even though the desk clerk was standing right there, just talking on the phone to someone.

Rakesh watched the taxi drive off, then he let out a sigh and walked back into the reception area.

Pete the lawyer was waiting by the desk, cuddling his briefcase tight. 'Excuse me, sir, can I—'

The desk clerk slammed the phone down. 'Here, Rakesh! Just got a call about a dog running around on the main road!'

## CHAPTER TWELVE

Phoebe Blackwell got out of her car and sucked in the cold night air, taking a minute to centre herself. Duddingston was a great wee place and she'd grown up here, but it was so emotionally cold.

She savoured the chill seeping into her bones, let it freshen up her head, which desperately needed it after that evening.

Lennon...

There was no way back from that.

But she knew there would be. Knew she'd let herself down again by letting him in through the door. She could only be strong for so long – and then she'd falter.

Same as every other time.

Maybe this time would be different.

Maybe this time her resolve wouldn't abandon her.

Maybe.

Probably wouldn't.

She got out her phone and checked for messages – just the usual shite in her group chats. Hardly had the time to open WhatsApp these days, let alone go in there and respond to the messages. She didn't have the time to *read* most of them, especially Chantal's – that girl seemed to be perpetually locked to her phone. Everything was an emoji, and mostly those crying laughing ones – hardly anything was *that* funny ever, and not several times per day.

Anyway.

The shop glowed bright in the dark evening. A real millstone around her neck, something she hadn't asked for but had got. Against her will.

She shivered again, then walked inside, into the heat.

Jen was working away in the corner, tying one of those hipster card-and-thread price tags over a big corner lamp.

Phoebe had *told* her not to do that – it had become *such* a cliché now. Those elegant price cards had taken ages to get right and looked really professional. Not to mention expensive to design and print.

Jen didn't look up from her work. 'Sorry, we're shut.'

'Are you?'

Jen looked over at the door and her eyes widened. 'Oh, Pheebs. Didn't think it'd be you.' She stood up. 'After that text you sent, I mean.'

Phoebe smiled so hard it hurt. 'I'm okay now.'

'Sure?'

'Sure.' Phoebe nodded, smiling *even* wider. 'You get yourself home, Jen.'

Jen fiddled with her phone.

'Can I give you a lift?'

'I'll call a taxi.' She put her phone to her ear. 'Hi, Maria. Collection at Sheridan Lighting. Oh, cool. See him soon, then.' She put it down, then grabbed her coat from the stand. 'Won't be long.'

'Surely you'd be cheaper owning your own car?'

'I don't trust car manufacturers. You know that.' Jen looked her up and down. 'How are you?'

'I've just been to yours, actually.' Phoebe held up the key. 'Let myself in. Hope that's okay?'

'Of course it is. *Mi casa es su casa*, and all that. I mean... It's not exactly under the best circumstances, but...' Jen held out her arms. 'Come here.'

Phoebe walked over and let her wee sister cuddle her. Wee only in being younger. She'd been taller since Phoebe was fourteen and Jen twelve. 'Fed Mr Kitty for you.'

Jen stroked her hair. 'You didn't need to feed him, but thank you.'

'Least I could do.'

Jen tightened her grip, like she could sense Phoebe was about to break off. 'Thought you were going to go to sleep?'

'Too keyed up for it. I put on a film but couldn't follow it. Then I tried reading my book, but I couldn't settle. And

I felt even more restless, knowing you were working in here. So I drove here to take over.'

Jen finally let go of her. 'It's not okay, is it? What happened, I mean.'

Phoebe hugged her sister tight again, rather than talk about it.

'Pheebs... Had he been drinking again?'

'It was nothing, Jen. A misunderstanding.' Phoebe broke off now and turned away.

Headlights scanned across the shop windows, though they didn't touch the brightness of the interior.

Phoebe playfully smacked Jen on the arm. 'There's your cab. Now, you get out of here. Need you on your A-game for the sale.'

Jen looked at her, mouth all twisted up. 'If you need me to stay and help, I'm happy to?'

'It's fine.' Phoebe shook her head. 'Can't have you doing all the work, can I?'

'Feels like you do.' Jen gave Phoebe another cuddle. 'I'm serious, aye? If he's been—'

'Thanks, Jen.'

Jen narrowed her eyes again. 'Come on. What happened?'

'Jen, I said it's fine. Listen, I've had a long night. I just want to get us ready for tomorrow.'

'What did he do?'

'Nothing.'

'Come on, Pheebs. You call me up, asking me to stay at

mine the day before our sale? Our first sale since we took over the place. That's not nothing. That's not fine.'

'It's not...' Phoebe sighed. 'He just threatened me, that's all.'

'He *threatened* you? That's a lot!'

'He didn't mean it.'

Jen smacked her on the arm. 'Fucking hell, Pheebs. Of course he meant it!'

Phoebe couldn't bring herself to look at her. 'I've got so much work to do.'

Jen grabbed her by the shoulders and stared into her eyes. 'Did you call the police?'

Phoebe tried to shrug her off but she was always the stronger one. She shook her head. 'A neighbour did. Probably that old witch next door or her idiot husband.'

'But you spoke to the cops?'

'Of course.'

Jen let out a deep breath. 'You daft biddy. No good comes from cooperating with the cops. Got to stick up for ourselves, Pheebs.'

'Not this conspiracy shit again...'

'It's not a conspiracy. The police are corrupt. Remember what happened to Uncle Stan?'

'Jen... I need to get on?'

'Okay, but if Lenny's being an arse, you could've got his brother to sort him out. Dylan's a good guy.'

'Dylan? He has absolutely no control over his brother.'

Jen shook her head. 'Never involve the filth, mark my words.'

Headlights flashed.

A horn beeped.

'Come on, you.' Phoebe patted Jen's arm. 'You're opening the shop first thing tomorrow, so you need to get home.'

Jen's mouth twitched. 'Look, there's not much left to do. Come home with me.'

'I've got the car, remember?' Phoebe stared hard at her. 'Besides, I want this to be perfect, okay? This is our first winter sale and it needs to be great.'

Jen shook her head. 'Okay, but you finish up, then come straight back to mine, okay?'

Phoebe nodded. 'Of course.'

Jen took a long hard look at her, then grabbed her bag from behind the till. She walked over to the door, then wagged a finger at Phoebe. 'I mean it.'

'I know. I'll finish up here, then head over. I've got a ton of stuff still to do. I'll be hours.'

'Hours?' Jen frowned, like all the work she'd put in was a waste. 'But I've done so much.'

'Yeah, sorry. It's looking great. But those Danish arseholes have let us down. Again. I need to get on top of that.'

'Told you, I can handle them.'

'Jen, that's not our agreement. You're front of house.'

'And if you're going to, do it in the morning.'

'Okay. I'll be right behind you. Half an hour at most.'

'If you're sure...'

'I am. I'll see you soon.'

Jen walked back over and pecked her on the cheek. She stared deep into her eyes, then something seemed to click inside her skull. 'I'll call you if you're not there, okay?' She walked back over to the door and left the shop.

Leaving Phoebe alone.

She let out a slow breath and took in the place, trying to assess how much work she had left to do before she could clear off. All she needed to do was implement her simple solution to the complex problem that was Jen's ability to go off on her own tangents, with her own ideas, which meant undoing half of what she'd done without her noticing.

The lights swept across the glass again as the taxi drove off.

She walked over and turned off the heating. That was something that needed to change. Half an hour before closing, maximum. The bills were through the roof.

Right... Where to start?

Phoebe grabbed the stack of cards, then started pricing up the remainder of items for the sale.

Jen's hipster card read:

~~£119~~

Now £79

Phoebe stapled the fancy card over it, giving a lot more

detail and – crucially – a barcode to scan through the till. What was the point in spending all that money on a stock inventory system if Jen just rang everything through under 'miscellaneous'?

Her phone chimed.

Bloody hell...

Jen pestering her. She was nothing if not persistent...

Another chime and this time Phoebe felt a chilling tingle deep in her guts. She knew exactly who that'd be – assigned him his own tone, a rising set of notes.

She walked over to her bag and pulled out her mobile, but didn't check the screen immediately. No, that needed another deep lungful of air.

Jen first:

> I mean it. Home soon! Jxx

Her heart was hammering in her chest.

Lennon knew not to message her, but he'd bloody done it.

> I'm really fucking sorry. Can we talk?

Phoebe stared at the message for a while, then shook her head and put her phone away.

What was it the sergeant said when he'd called her?

Investigative release.

Don't speak, don't communicate.

She hated this. It went against everything she believed in.

Sod it.

She picked up her phone and tapped out a reply:

> Police said we're not to speak for two weeks. Where are you?

She put her phone down again, then attached a price tag to a table lamp. It would look nice in the corner of the kitchen, once they'd finished the refit.

Christ.

That felt a million years away now.

And it wouldn't happen, would it?

Or if it did, it'd just be for them to sell the place and not live in it.

Her phone chimed again and she immediately felt a stinging deep in her guts, almost before her brain acknowledged it.

This was wrong. She shouldn't be doing this.

And whatever Jen said, she knew she could trust the police.

The ones who'd come around were nice. They chatted like old friends. She knew they wanted the best for her.

Phoebe picked up her phone again and checked the message:

> At Dylan's. I'm really sorry, babe. I just want to see you. Where are you?

She slammed her phone down and went back to work.

Snapped a card onto an uplighter.

Then one onto a pair of table lamps that looked like a cute couple.

She reached over to a tall lamp to—

She stumbled and fell forward, tipping the lamp over.

She caught herself against the wall, caught the lamp stem before it tipped over or scraped the paintwork.

Bloody hell.

She'd dug her palm into a screw that wasn't quite flush with the wall but had still been painted over. Dad should've removed it. Hell, she should've done.

She set it down again and took a deep breath.

Lennon was really doing a number on her and he wasn't even here!

She grabbed her phone and stabbed out a message:

> I'm at work. This needs to wait until tomorrow.

She sent it, then looked back through the last few.

She definitely shouldn't have said where she was.

> Lennon, I need to think a few things through. The way you spoke to me tonight wasn't cool. At all. Do you understand?

She stood there, looking at the phone. Waiting for his message to arrive.

> Said I'm sorry, Pheebs. Just… I love you so much. It gets to me at times.

She couldn't help but shake her head again. She started typing.

> I get it. Let's just cool down and chat tomorrow. Okay? x

She put her phone on silent then stuck it face down on the other side of the till. Out of reach.

She picked up the stack of tags, down to the last six, then started attaching them to the lamps around the window. The main part of the display for tomorrow.

Bloody Lennon was still living rent-free in her head.

God, he had a mortgage in there.

She stapled the last card, then checked her phone.

> Cops said I wasn't to speak to you.

> That's up to me, okay? Let's chat tomorrow. Sleep tight.

> You too. I miss you.

Phoebe put her phone back in her bag. Out of sight and all that.

Life must've been so much simpler before these bloody things. You couldn't threaten someone as effectively with a postcard, could you?

She looked over at the door, where Jen had been standing just a few moments ago. Should've gone with her. Should leave now and sit with her. Talk it all through. Let Jen in, for once.

She started putting the final touches on the display by the till, making sure it was all *just* right, then stood back. 'That'll do…' She grabbed her phone and walked over to the door, then turned off the lights.

It was pitch dark inside. And even darker outside.

She opened the door and let the freezing air in. Then realised her bag was still on the counter.

'Shite.' She walked through the dark shop to get it. She dropped her phone into the bag.

Then got it out again.

> I love you.

Bloody Lennon…

A rattle came from the back room.

What the hell was that?

Phoebe tiptoed over to the door, then eased it open. Her heart was pounding in her ears.

Nothing.

Then the rattle started again.

'Hello?'

The rattle stopped.

She stepped into the room, full of boxes and lamps.

The ancient stock computer Dad swore by, older than

Jen and just as flaky. Yet another thing she needed to replace.

Nobody there, just a box slowly tipping over. Happened all the time.

And because she was so on edge, she was imagining the worst.

She was just imagining it, wasn't she?

She walked back through and made sure the door was shut, then grabbed her phone and typed out a message.

> I love you too, Lenny. But it's not easy, is it?

She didn't send it.

She needed to speak to Jen about this. And be open to any options here.

Maybe divorce wasn't the worst outcome.

But he always valued her sharing her feelings. Maybe it'd make a difference.

Sod it.

She hit send, then stood there rubbing her forehead. Regretting the hell out of sending it.

A phone chimed in the darkness.

Between her and the door.

Someone was in there with her.

# CHAPTER THIRTEEN

Rakesh drove slowly along Niddrie Mains Road, scanning both sides of the street.

Slow enough to get a honk from behind.

Took a special kind of person to honk a police car...

And to overtake him with a blast of the horn.

Rakesh noted the plate of the Subaru, but didn't change his speed, searching the roadside for the dog. Maybe the dog didn't even exist. Maybe it had been found by its owner, or taken by a well-meaning member of the public to the cat and dog home down by Seafield.

He didn't want to think about the worst outcome.

Rakesh slowed at the junction and pulled up. Left was the police station and Duddingston. Straight ahead was deeper into Niddrie. To the right, the Pit Heid pub was still open and trading. Hopefully it was just filled with Johnnie and his mates, with the gang of neds heeding his advice to bugger off and keep buggered off.

Rakesh didn't feel comfortable calling them neds, despite that being the term everyone used. It demeaned them and he knew as well as anyone the negative power of reducing someone to a label.

There.

A wee West Highland terrier scurried around in the undergrowth outside the beer garden. It squatted to do a pee – at least, Rakesh thought that's what it was doing. He had no idea about dogs, other than you needed to completely dominate them.

A lesson he'd learned the hard way in his stint – his right hand still had the bite marks.

No sign of an owner and it certainly matched the description of the missing one, so he pulled in and got out into wispy rain.

A young man appeared from the beer garden, hooded top and baggy clothes, arms waving as he chased the wee dog. 'Come *here*!'

Of course, the dog ran towards Rakesh.

He opened the car's back door and put on his best doggy voice. 'Want to go for a drive, boy?'

The wee dog jumped right up onto the back seat. It stood there, mouth open, tail wagging, looking right at him.

Rakesh closed the door and let out a relieved breath. The worst outcome hadn't happened – and that felt like the best one had. 'Thank you for stopping him, sir.' He turned to face the dog's saviour.

Up close, Rakesh could now see the man's face.

Keegan, the ned who'd elbowed Bell and started the whole thing. Smoothing down his moustache.

Definitely a breach of the peace case.

Keegan's eyes bulged, then he swung around and raced away, his long legs putting distance between them.

*Spectacular...*

Rakesh checked the back door was shut, then sprinted off after Keegan, flicking on his BWV as he ran. The bloody awful shoes and the too-tight trousers hampered his speed – Keegan had such a head start on him and was increasing it with every step.

Keegan turned right into a modern housing estate, near where Helen tasered the other ned, the one whose act of spitting on Johnnie had lit the whole powder keg and who'd shot the Roman candle at Liam.

To win this, Rakesh knew he had to outsmart Keegan, so he took the diagonal path and gained some ground on him.

Keegan shot along a lane running between new houses, way too far ahead of him.

Rakesh stopped and didn't follow him.

Instead, he stood there, listening to Keegan's footsteps cannoning off the buildings and receding into the distance. Then slowing and growing slightly louder.

*Excellent...*

Rakesh walked back the way they'd run and waited on the corner, back against a garage wall.

A Toyota was parked haphazardly, but faced away so the wing mirror gave a good view back down the street.

Sure enough, Keegan was jogging towards him.

Rakesh waited, pressing back against the garage wall.

Keegan's footsteps slowed to a jog.

Rakesh waited, drawing his taser.

In the mirror, Keegan was walking now, scanning the area slowly.

Rakesh waited, getting the taser ready to fire.

A cough, then Keegan stepped past him.

Rakesh aimed the taser at Keegan's back. The red targeting lasers bounced up and down the hoodie. 'Keegan Tait, you're under arrest.'

Keegan swung around, then rushed towards Rakesh, fists raised. 'Am I fu—'

Rakesh fired the taser and it hit Keegan's jacket.

But that was the only dart that stuck, driven into his shoulder.

The second dart dangled free on the ground, sparking noisily.

Keegan looked down at it and laughed. 'Thought you'd try to electro—'

Rakesh lurched forward and stabbed the taser into Keegan's left hip.

The circuit completed.

Keegan started shaking, then fell forward and landed on the ground.

# CHAPTER FOURTEEN

Rakesh got out of the car and nodded at Ella. 'There you go.'

'Hello! Who's a good little doggie?' She picked up the dog from the back seat of the car and its tiny legs wriggled, like it was running on the air. 'Oh, you're a feisty wee devil.'

Helen sat behind the wheel of the squad car, laughing as she talked to someone on the phone. Probably about the scene unfolding in front of her.

'Thank you, Ella.' Rakesh smiled at her. 'Can you return him to his owner, please?'

'I think he's a she, Sarge, but I will do.' She kissed the wee bugger on the head, then carried her over to Helen's squad car and got into the front passenger seat with her.

Rakesh watched the car drive off with Ella tickling the dog's ears, then looked around at Keegan. 'Meanwhile, I need to find out who owns you...' He opened the back door and helped Keegan out, leading him by the handcuffs into the station's back door.

Keegan swerved to the left and clattered his shoulder off the doorframe. 'Fuck sake.'

'Easy does it.' Rakesh tightened his grip on Keegan's arm as he walked him up to the counter.

As ever, Wilson was behind the desk, yawning into a cup of acrid-smelling coffee. He set it down and stood up to finish his yawn. 'Busy shift for you, Rakesh.'

'Wish it wasn't.'

'Busy ones go the quickest.' Wilson smiled at Keegan. 'Name?'

'Keegan.'

'Surname or first name?'

'Keegan Tait.'

'Got a middle name?'

'Eh.'

'How do you spell "eh"?'

'Funny.'

'Do you have a middle name or not?'

'Nope.'

'Join the club, pal.' Wilson scribbled something on the form. 'Current address?'

'My mate Shaft's sofa.'

'And what's this Shaft's address?'

Keegan looked away. 'Not supposed to be living there, so I'm not fucking telling you.'

'Has he got a name?'

'Told you.' Keegan frowned. 'Shaft.'

Wilson stuck his tongue into his cheek. 'And is that a first name, a surname or a terrible nickname for a white man?'

'Shaft ain't white.'

'My apologies, then.' Wilson rolled his eyes. 'It's not just a terrible nickname, it's a racist one too. Do you happen to know this Shaft's real name?'

Keegan shrugged. 'Search me.'

'That'll happen in due course.' Wilson tapped his pen off the desk. 'How about your mum's address?'

'She's dead.'

'What about—'

'Dad's dead too.'

Wilson sighed. 'No fixed abode, then.' He looked up. 'Makes you homeless. Given that's your situation, sure you could get on a shortlist for a flat from the council.' He paused, then frowned. 'Though I'm guessing you'll be given accommodation courtesy of the King for a while.'

Keegan scowled at him. 'The *King*?'

'King Charles. The third.'

'What happened to the Queen?'

'She died. A while ago now.'

'Fuck me hard and fast. Never heard that.'

'In the name of the wee man.' Wilson glowered back. 'How can you not have heard?'

'Search me.'

'What about at school?'

'Haven't been for years.' Keegan cleared his throat. 'Why's the King putting me up?'

Wilson braced himself against the desk. 'You ever heard the phrase "His Majesty's Pleasure"?'

Keegan screwed up his lips. 'What did you say, boomer?'

'Boomer. Brilliant.' Wilson laughed. 'It means you'll be in prison.'

Keegan sneered at him. 'Fuck off.'

'Charming.' Wilson went back to his form. 'Not my fault you don't pay attention at school.'

'Fuck do you know about it, cunt? You did so well at school, why are you working here?'

Instead of rage, mischief twinkled in Wilson's eyes. 'You wouldn't believe how many times I hear those exact words from identikit wee jobbies like you.'

Keegan looked around at Rakesh. 'Did you hear what he called me? A wee jobbie!'

Wilson looked down at his feet. 'Oh, jings, I must've forgot to start recording.' He reached down and the camera's red light switched to green. 'Here we go. As I was saying, you wouldn't believe the similar stories I hear from young gentlemen in your situation. All variations on the same tired theme.'

Keegan snarled at him. 'Prick.'

Wilson tapped his pen off the form, the nib clacking in a really annoying way.

Keegan's focus was trained on that pen bouncing up and down.

Wilson clicked the pen and set it down. 'So, both your parents are dead. How old are you? Thirty? Forty?'

'Cheeky bastard. Nineteen.'

Wilson's eyebrows shot up. 'Man, that must've been some paper round.'

Rakesh gave a brief warning glare to Wilson, then focused on Keegan. 'How old were you when they died?'

'Don't know.' Keegan sniffed. 'Mum died a few years back. Old man a wee bit further back.'

Rakesh held his gaze until he looked away. 'It's not your fault.'

'What is?'

'What's happened to you. To put you on this path. It's not on you.'

Keegan nodded, like he was heeding some harsh life lesson. Then he looked at Rakesh with a gleam in his eyes. 'That mean I can go now?'

Rakesh shook his head. 'No. Not after you did what you did. You struck a police officer. Broke another's nose. Then you ran off.' He paused, drilling his glare deep into the young man's soul. 'Oh and you lit two fireworks which an acquaintance fired at another officer, causing severe damage.'

Keegan shook his head. 'Police brutality, man.'

'You're not interested in Gabriel's wellbeing, are you?'

'Eh?'

'Your friend Happy Meal. Gabriel McInvar.'

'Oh, right.' Keegan shrugged. 'Should I be?'

'He's been asking after you.'

'Man...'

'How did he come by that name?'

'Ordered a Happy Meal in Maccy Dees once.'

Aye, the shittier the nickname, the harder it stuck to you. 'It's only because of that dog that I caught you.'

Keegan looked up at the heavens. 'Fucking dog. Shouldn't have saved it... Almost got run over.'

'Do you like dogs, Keegan?'

'Love them.' Keegan stared at his feet. 'Mum had cats when I was wee. Filthy wee sods. I like dogs, though. They're easy to understand. Pack mentality, right? You dominate them. Show them who's boss. Own them. Then you command absolute respect.'

Rakesh gave the kid a kind smile. 'That's what I've heard.'

'Dad had a dog. Called him Bastard. One of those junkie XL things.'

Wilson's laugh was like a snapped bone. 'You mean a bully XL?'

Keegan shrugged. 'Aye. One of them. What's a junkie XL?'

'Did that Elvis remix. "A Little Less Conversation".'

'What the fuck are you talking about, boomer?' Keegan shook his head. 'Bastard was a braw dog, like. Strong and fierce, but Dad put him in his place.'

'Must be tough, losing him.'

Keegan nodded. 'Uncle didn't want Bastard when I went to stay with him, so he went to the kennel, eh?'

'Meant your dad.'

Keegan brushed at his cheek. 'Oh, aye. Right. Saw him in prison a few times. Mum took us in. Didn't say much to me. Seemed a bit beaten down, like. And when he got out, he went straight to the pub with his mates. Didn't even come to see me.' He swallowed hard. 'Got into a fight with this squaddie in a pub on Leith Walk. And he died. Or so the story goes.'

'Was that after your mum—'

'Aye.' The way Keegan snapped it out showed real pain, somewhere deep in what passed for a soul.

Rakesh needed to stop thinking that way. At Keegan's age, he was still the product of his upbringing and environment. He was as much a victim of the tragedies that happened to him. Losing his parents so young, for instance.

But he was on the precipice – the tragedies had started becoming things he was responsible for, things he did to people, like poor Liam.

To avoid worse things happening in future, Rakesh knew he should show him as much kindness and compassion as he'd accept.

God, this job could crush your soul if you let it…

'What about your uncle? Could you stay—'

'Dead too. Got stabbed near the Pit Heid a few months ago. Hence me staying with Shaft.'

'Here you go.' Wilson presented the form for Keegan to sign, then stood up tall. 'Sign there, young man.'

Keegan looked at the paperwork. 'This is *bull*shit.'

'Okay. Read it, weep, then sign.'

Keegan stared around the room, shaking his head like he was the innocent party. 'You're going to put me in jail for fighting off police brutality?'

'Defending yourself is one thing, Sonny Jim. Kicking a man when he's down with a group of your mates is quite the other.' Wilson folded his arms. 'You'll just be in the cell for an hour while I run checks on you. Assuming there are no warrants or previous crimes, then we can consider letting you go.' He looked at Rakesh. 'Right, Sarge?'

'That's correct.'

Keegan finally did as he was told.

Wilson snatched the form back before Keegan could damage it. 'Come on.' He led him through the door into the cells.

Rakesh followed them into the long corridor, with ten royal blue doors on each side. Whoever designed this had been a bit on the optimistic side with their maximum capacity, but Rakesh had to hand it to them – it was getting close to full tonight.

Wilson shut the door and twisted the key.

Keegan looked at Rakesh through the bars. 'You seriously going to put me in jail for lighting a firework?'

'You put yourself there, Keegan. There's no remorse there, no regret or surprise. They were deliberate acts.'

'I didn't fire it. And you're going to stick *me* in jail?'

Rakesh nodded. 'Technically, it'll be the procurator fiscal who prosecutes you. And a jury who will decide on your guilt. And the judge who will determine your sentence.' He left a pause, watching the technical language hit the mark in a way the other stuff hadn't. 'I saw what you did to one of my constables, Keegan. We've got it on video. It was pretty severe. You didn't just react, you tried to kill him. If I hadn't stopped you, you'd be on a murder charge.'

Keegan looked away for a few seconds, then back at Rakesh. 'You expect a thanks?'

'Changing your ways would be thank you enough.'

'Is that cop okay?' The small voice came from the next cell.

Rakesh stepped aside and looked through the bars.

Happy Meal – AKA Gabriel McInvar – sat there, knees up to his chin. Shining blue eyes looked at Rakesh, then away again.

'He's in hospital, so no – he's not okay.'

Those eyes were back on him, wider now. 'From *that*?'

'The Roman candle got into his underwear. And set fire to the fabric, which burned his skin. And there are internal wounds.'

'*How?*'

'PC Inglis removed his trousers in an attempt at

putting out the fire. He'll be lucky to get out of hospital soon. I imagine he'll probably require skin grafts.'

Happy Meal gritted his teeth, then looked back down at the floor. The harsh truth of gang life could hit you like a brick in the face. Right there, he looked so young, many years younger than his supposed eighteen. He huffed out a sigh. 'Fuck sake, man. Just a bit of fun, you know? Didn't know hitting someone in the arse with a rocket could hurt them like *that*.'

'A man intends the natural course of his actions.'

Happy Meal looked over at Wilson. 'Eh?'

'You fired a rocket at a cop, son. You knew what was going to happen.'

'Just supposed to be a bit of banter, you know? Going to prison for *that*? Fucking bullshit, man. Total bullshit.'

Wilson laughed. 'Did you expect to get knighted for it?'

Happy Meal shook his head. 'Can't do prison, man.'

'You'll get used to it. The first few months are the toughest.'

Happy Meal's eyes bulged. '*Months?*'

'First offence with no previous. Assuming your lawyer's smart enough to persuade you to plead guilty and you're smart enough to listen.' Wilson looked around the corridor, as though checking for cobwebs. 'I'd say you're going to be inside for a year.'

Happy Meal leaned forward and rested his head on

the concrete. 'There's no way I'm going to jail for that, boomer.'

'Ah, Gen Z.' Wilson laughed. 'Consequences happen to other people.'

'In prison for a year...' Happy Meal turned away and started quietly sobbing. 'Fuck.'

Rakesh knew crocodile tears when he saw them. He knew an attempt to swindle free of a crime. And that's what he saw here.

Wasn't it?

Or was the sheer magnitude of the situation hitting him?

Happy Meal had leapt over that precipice and his life was now in free fall.

Rakesh locked eyes with Wilson. 'Book him. Assault causing bodily harm.' Liam's screams would never leave him. 'Oh, and an assault on a constable in the execution of their duty.'

'Will do, Sarge.'

Rakesh took one last look at Keegan, then walked off out of the area, leaving Happy Meal silently weeping.

Footsteps followed him.

Wilson whistled. 'Guy like that doesn't learn a lesson the hundredth time you teach him it.'

# CHAPTER FIFTEEN

Rakesh walked into the main reception area. The couple from earlier were now standing at the desk, locked in a discussion with the desk clerk. He looked back at the door to the processing area and the cells, where Keegan and Happy Meal were being dealt blows they'd hopefully learn from. But probably wouldn't.

'Rakesh.' Asher stood in the other doorway, arms folded. The harsh light hid his eyes under his thick brow ridge. 'Good work.'

'What do you mean, sir?'

'Keegan Tait.' Asher gestured at the door to the processing area. 'I watched that. You maintained calmness throughout that whole thing. Bet he was calling you all the names under the sun during transport.'

'And a few above the sun.'

Asher smiled. 'Indeed. But you kept the wee bastard onside, didn't you? And you got his confession on the booking camera.'

Rakesh gave him a shrug. 'All part of the job, sir.'

'Aye, sure. *And* you rescued a wee dog.'

'Keegan rescued the dog, sir. I secured it and kept it in my car while I chased him and caught him.'

'Should build a statue outside for you.' The cheeky bastard grinned wide. 'Guess everyone's got to have their own personal kryptonite, eh? Didn't expect Keegan's to be a wee pooch. Even hard bastards love their dogs. How's it going with the Roman candle wielder?'

Rakesh shrugged. 'I think he's resigned to his fate.'

'Good.'

The side door opened and Bell strutted in with gauze stuffed up his nose.

Asher gasped at him. 'Jesus, George, what the hell happened to you?'

Bell caressed his nose. 'A&E waiting times habbened to be.' He tugged out the bloody gauze and flung it in the bin. 'Horrible stuff.'

Asher arched a thin eyebrow mounted on his caveman skull. 'I meant, what happened to your nose?'

'That wee scrotum Keegan Tait hit me.'

Asher smiled. 'Well, the good news is he's in processing.'

Bell beamed wide. 'Oh, that *is* good news.'

Asher clapped Rakesh on the arm. 'All thanks to this man here. And a wee Scotty dog.'

Bell looked at Asher like he'd gone completely insane, then smiled at Rakesh. 'Good work, Sarge.'

'All part of the job, eh?' Rakesh narrowed his eyes and gestured at his nose. 'You're okay, though?'

'Aye, Sarge. Not my first rodeo, mind. Not the first time I've—'

'Please, God, no.' Asher raised a hand. 'I don't need to hear how you used to be a boxer.'

'Aye, aye.' Bell snorted. 'Just have to wait for it to stop bleeding, apparently.' He patted his nose and winced. 'Spoke to young Liam when I was in the hospital, though. Kid's not in a good way. Ton of painkillers, but ouch. Doubt we'll see him this side of Christmas.'

Asher shook his head, jaw clenched. 'Last thing I wanted to hear...'

'Sorry, sir, but it's better out than in.' Bell grinned at Rakesh. 'Right, Shunty?'

The words hit Rakesh like a taser, the needle dug into his eye and his balls.

He shut his eyes – he'd been hiding that nickname from them for two months now.

He'd known it was only going to be a matter of time before it got out, but...

He hadn't so much thought he'd got away with it as just actually forgotten about it.

Stupid.

Really bloody stupid.

Asher was frowning at him. '*Shunty*?'

Bell nodded. 'One of the lads from the Edinburgh MIT was in seeing Liam at the same time. Says everyone in the Borders calls Rakesh "Shunty".'

Asher looked at Rakesh. 'How did you earn that soubriquet?'

'Crashed a pool car into a wall.' Rakesh shrugged like it was no big deal, then laughed, like that'd help. 'Well, a bridge.'

Asher laughed like it was a massive deal. 'How the *hell* did you manage that?'

Rakesh shrugged again. 'It was icy. We were transporting a suspect and a colleague let him get away.' He looked at Bell, his gaze narrow. 'George, you can go and get your piece now. The rest had theirs earlier. And you wanted it around now, anyway.'

Bell nodded with military precision. 'Aye, cheers, Shunty.' He coughed. 'I mean, Sarge.'

Asher clapped him on the back like he was congratulating a massive dog. 'Don't make me remind everyone what you did in your first week…'

'Aye, aye.' Bell scuttled off towards the locker rooms.

Rakesh followed his path, even stared at the door as it shut behind him and rattled. Then looked over at Asher. 'What *did* he do?'

Asher walked over and leaned in close. 'Some wee bastards had swiped a few crates of a certain tonic wine made in Devon from an off licence in the Jewel. While we searched for said wee bastards, we left Bell guarding the crime scene, sitting in ECC15. Lovely hot day, right at the end of his first shift rotation. And naturally, Bell fell asleep. And, of course, said wee bastards returned. Poor owner lost twice as much stock as they did in the first break-in.'

'So they broke into the place with him sitting in front?'

'Exactly that. Brazen wee bastards. Unbelievable, eh?' Asher bellowed. 'Called him "Nytol" for a year after that.'

Rakesh couldn't help but laugh. 'Nytol. I love it.'

Asher smirked at his own joke. 'Not that Bell needs to take any. Arsehole can kip anywhere. On young Dean's stag down in Harrogate last year, he slept in the luggage rack back all the way from York.' He frowned. 'Oh, I forgot to say. There's someone waiting in my office to see you.'

# CHAPTER SIXTEEN

Rakesh walked along the corridor, clutching his box of sandwiches. He was starving now – his guts had been aching all day, but he needed some eggy goodness to sort it all out. He knocked on the door to Asher's office, waited a few seconds before opening it.

Acting DCI Rob Marshall was sitting behind the desk, twatting about on his phone. He hadn't got any smaller – or any less handsome.

Rakesh stood by the door. 'Rob?'

Marshall looked up. 'Rakesh. There you are. Beginning to think I'd been stood up.' He looked Rakesh up and down. 'Bloody hell, you look like a sausage bursting out of the skin.'

Rakesh stared down at his bulging polo shirt. 'It's not that bad, is it?'

'It's not that good, either.'

Rakesh sat down in front of the desk. 'When the boss said there was someone to see me, I wondered who it'd be. Didn't think it'd be you.' He held up his sandwich box. 'Haven't had my piece yet. Mind if I eat?'

'Be my guest.'

'Starving.' Rakesh opened his box and pulled out the first sandwich.

Marshall scowled at him. 'What the *hell* is that?'

'Don't *you* start.' Rakesh bit into it and chewed. 'Spectacular.'

Truth was, it was a bit on the warm side considering it'd been out of the fridge for so long, but it was better than nothing.

Marshall scowled at him. 'Is that an *omelette* sandwich?'

'You've never had one?'

'Never even thought it was possible.' Marshall frowned. 'Isn't that just French toast gone wrong?'

'Gone very right, you mean.'

'Thought you were vegan?'

'I lapsed. Cheese and eggs are very hard to give up for good. These came from a friend's flock in her garden, so hard to get any more ethical.' Rakesh took ages chewing his mouthful, long enough for Marshall to hopefully forget what he was eating. 'What brings you up here, then?'

'Over actually.' Marshall picked up a bottle of water

and twisted the cap. 'Just been over at Kirsten's flat in Gorgie.' He held up a hand. 'Of course. You've been there.' He took a swig of water. 'We've got a ton of stuff to chuck out before we sell it.'

'You're selling?'

'She is. Kirst's taking our cat to my mum's for a few weeks while we do all the showings. Assuming it'll sell.'

'Two-bed flat there will shift quickly.'

'Wish I had your confidence.' Marshall frowned. 'When did Zlatan become *our* cat rather than just mine? And when did it become *our* flat?'

Rakesh grinned. 'Must be love.' He smiled as he chewed. 'Are you moving to the Borders, then?'

Marshall nodded. 'That's the plan. Kirst's just taken a job down there too. Need to sell our places first. My flat in London's been stuck on the market, but I've finally got a bidder. And there's no chain this time.'

'So you are getting serious, then?'

Marshall shrugged. 'Been that way for a while, I suppose.' He cleared his throat. 'Anyway, I'm not here for a chitchat, as nice as it is. I thought this'd be better done in person, so I checked with Control, only to find you're on duty. So here I am.'

Rakesh put his sandwich down. He felt that throbbing deep in his stomach. The same one he'd got going into a meeting room with Marshall's father a few months ago, when he'd been cast out from Professional Standards. His mouth was all dry and the sandwich caught in his throat.

'Would've done this at the start of your shift, but I've been in meetings in Tulliallan all day.' Marshall screwed the bottle cap back on. 'Bottom line is, DCS Potter is still in favour of you getting the gig in the Borders MIT.'

The throbbing stopped and he could swallow again. 'That sounds good.' Rakesh picked up his sandwich again, then dropped it. 'I'm sensing a but, though?'

Marshall looked away. 'But she made it clear frontline policing has to be the priority.'

'I see. So I'm stuck here?'

Marshall held up a hand. 'That's just in the short term, Rakesh. Corstorphine and Craigmillar are both short-staffed, whereas the Borders MIT is holding its own compared to the other MITs. Probably because we're not that busy. And Edinburgh has people being decapitated with old Japanese swords.'

'Katanas.'

'What?'

'Old Japanese swords. They're called katanas.' Rakesh finished chewing, then scowled. 'Rob, that sounds like I'm not getting the job.'

'No. It's just... Delayed. And it's been decided the last two months have been good for your development, so another four won't hurt.'

'Four?'

'You'll be deemed to be street legal, then.'

'Funny way of putting it.'

'Here's the plan. The role's going to be open for three

months, then you'll have to work the month's notice period.' Marshall leaned forward and took another sip of water. 'Truth is, Rakesh, I could really do with you now. The DS who's acting up to DS just now isn't exactly setting the heather alight. *Way* too green. And there aren't exactly many other candidates down there. Last thing I want to do is go cap in hand to the Edinburgh or Glasgow lot.' He raised an eyebrow. 'Best way to inherit someone else's problem. That's how we ended up with Struan in the first place...' He looked away and snorted.

'How's that all going, Rob?'

'It's not settled, if that's what you mean. I want to move on them, but people above me or to the side don't want me to. Since when did the drugs squad take precedence over the MITs?' Marshall sank the rest of the water, then dumped the bottle into the bin. 'I want you as a DS, Rakesh. And I'm prepared to wait. I'm just sorry you have to, that's all, but this will be good for you.'

Rakesh stuffed the rest of his second sandwich in his mouth and ate it far too quickly. The room was roasting – he needed to get out of there. Drink some water. Stand in the cold air. Think about something else for a bit.

Marshall stared down his nose at him. 'You okay there, Rakesh?'

'I'm fine.' But he couldn't look at Marshall.

'I don't want you going all catatonic on me again.'

Rakesh glanced at him, made eye contact, then looked away again just as quickly. 'I'm sorry. That was a shock.'

'And this isn't?'

'No. I think I expected this.'

'Okay, but it's not—'

Someone knocked on the door.

Rakesh stood up a bit too quickly. 'Come in!'

Marshall glared at him – this wasn't finished, at least not in his eyes.

Ella entered the room, looking frazzled. 'Sorry to interrupt, Sarge. It's just, we've got a report of a break-in.'

## CHAPTER SEVENTEEN

Rakesh blasted down the long road from the station towards Duddingston village, his squad car's blue lights casting the street in a hard glow. No siren, but ECC17 was behind him like they were drag racers in some old film. He took a hard left then weaved through the cobbled streets until he spotted the address. He bumped up onto the pavement and got out, leaving the blue lights on.

He swung around, took in the vicinity.

Sheridan Lighting

Very fancy-looking place. Ancient stone. Those old lights that should really be fuelled by paraffin. Four floor-to-ceiling windows, all dark, and a closed door in the middle beneath the sign. Posters in the window advertised:

> Winter Sale
> Starts 1st December
> For two weeks

That date felt like ages away but the hard truth was it was tomorrow.

Rakesh checked his watch and saw that tomorrow was actually only an hour and twenty minutes away.

How the hell did it get to December?

Maybe Marshall was right – maybe the four months would pass by as quickly as the first two had.

Trouble was, now Bell knew Rakesh had a nickname, he had a pretty good feeling for how it would go.

Ella and Helen got out of the other car and slipped on their caps like they were performing in synchronised policing at the Olympics.

Helen stepped up to the door and peered inside, but didn't say anything.

Ella was looking around the place, casting her gaze on everything but the shop.

A flash of headlights caught them, then Bell's car turned up next, parking in the middle of the road. He got out, still tapping at his nose.

Daft sod really shouldn't be on duty, should he?

Rakesh pointed at him. 'George, can you check around

the back?' At Ella. 'Can you guard the front?' He waited for a nod, then at Helen. 'You stay right behind me.'

'Sarge.' Helen stepped up to the second window. Up close, it was obvious the glass had been smashed in. Most of it was scattered inside the shop, covering old floor tiles, but a few shards had spilled onto the pavement.

Rakesh stood there, watching Helen brush the edges with her baton. 'Has anyone contacted the owner?'

Helen nodded. 'Control are on it, Sarge.'

'Okay, let's see what's happened inside, then.' Rakesh used his baton to clear the remaining glass from the window surround, then followed Helen into the shop.

The place was pitch black, some mirrors picking up reflections as Rakesh switched on his torch. He swept it around the place, across an army of sleeping lamps. He traced the beam along the walls, then walked over to flick on the light switch.

The place glowed bright. So bright Rakesh had to shut his eyes.

The lamps ran across a huge range from spindly modern brass things to spindly ancient brass things, through a spectrum of floor lamps of all sorts of appearances. Not a surface was without a lamp or six. The walls were filled with uplighters of all shapes and styles.

Helen scanned around the place like a keen shopper on the first morning of the sale. She leaned in to whisper. 'Some lights are clearly missing, Sarge.'

Rakesh saw where she meant – over in the corner,

there was a noticeable space between two floor lamps. He checked around the shop and nowhere else matched that pattern. 'Assuming they're not just gaps.'

'True. We need to—'

'Sarge!' Bell's voice roared through from an open door behind the till.

Rakesh rushed through and stepped into a back room.

A door on the left of the room hung open.

Bell stood in the corner beside an ancient computer, beige monitor sitting on a beige case with a beige mouse and keyboard in front. He stepped aside and let Rakesh see what had made him call them through.

Phoebe Blackwell lay there, her skull caved in. Her clothes were covered with fragments of ceramic from the smashed-in light discarded on the floor next to her.

## CHAPTER EIGHTEEN

Rakesh put his hands on his hips and surveyed the scene.

Helen taped off the area, struggling with the wind and rain. 'For crying out loud!' She bit the tape and wrapped it around a railing. 'This is *impossible*.'

Nearby, Ella was talking to a man in a dressing gown and slippers.

'Remember when the sales were in January.' The man shook his head like his son had just failed his Highers. For the second time. 'Now everything's always on sale, all year round. Makes you wonder how businesses make any money.'

His wife stood next to him, dressed in yoga gear, with a thick rugby jumper pulled over the top. 'Volume game, Colin. Volume game.'

Colin scowled at her. 'A light shop in Duddingston isn't a volume game.'

'True.'

'So why did you say it was?'

'Just that if stuff's always on sale, they're playing a volume game. Those lassies clearly aren't. That's the first sale since they took over. And it's only lasting a fortnight.'

'Mary, what the hell are you talking about?'

Rakesh walked away from them towards the shop. He peered inside, but nobody from the MIT or forensics had arrived, so it was just Bell in there.

What a mess.

On so many levels.

Someone would no doubt blame them for letting Lennon Blackwell go. And it was hard to escape the feeling that the most likely scenario was Lennon had followed through on his threat to kill his wife.

Rakesh got out his phone and called Lennon.

'We're sorry but the number you've dialled is unavailable. Please leave a message after the tone.'

Rakesh waited for the beep, which took longer than he expected. 'Mr Blackwell, it's Sergeant Siyal from Police Scotland. We spoke to you earlier this evening. I'd appreciate you giving me a call back when you get a second. Thanks.' He left his number, then ended the call.

And didn't know what to do.

He stood there, trying to figure it all out. Trying to

work out if Lennon Blackwell had done this. And where the hell he was.

He tried calling Phoebe's mobile.

A phone rang inside the shop.

Rakesh stepped back inside and tracked the ringing to behind the till, where the phone lay face down.

He stared at it for a few seconds.

His instinct was to pick it up and bag it, but he wasn't a detective. That'd been made abundantly clear on several occasions.

Still, if Lennon had done this, wouldn't he have taken the phone? He'd more than likely know the device's passcode or at least be able to successfully guess it after a few attempts.

He suspected his wife was having an affair, so it stood to reason he'd want to find who it was.

And then find him.

*Shite.*

A patrol car pulled up outside the shop.

Rakesh left the phone where it was and walked back out.

Asher was getting out into the rain.

Rakesh met him and took him to the side. 'Sir, I take full responsibility for this.'

'I see.' Asher looked over at the shop. 'Did Lennon drive off?'

'He didn't drive, sir. He hailed a taxi.'

Asher sniffed. 'And he got that taxi right bloody here.'

He sighed. 'Still. We did the right thing. We can't keep everyone in who's had an argument with their wife, otherwise we'd have nobody but single people on the street. Going to face a few questions now, though.'

'Happy to help answer them, sir.'

'Damn right you...' Asher stopped dead. 'What the hell?'

Rakesh spotted the ambulance pulling up behind Asher's car.

Asher glowered at it. 'An ambulance? But she—'

'She's still alive, sir.' Rakesh pointed to the ambulance. 'Paramedics rather than pathologist.'

Asher seemed to slump with relief.

The paramedics charged past them into the shop, lugging a gurney behind them.

Asher watched them go. 'What the hell was Phoebe Blackwell doing here?'

'She owns the shop, sir.'

Asher glowered. 'Maiden name?'

'Right.'

Asher swallowed. 'What the hell happened here?'

'It appears someone beat her up with a lamp. We found a broken one in the back. Ceramic base. Her body was covered in fragments. They must've thought they'd killed her, but she's still breathing.' Rakesh pointed over to Helen. 'George and Helen kept her alive, basically.'

Asher sucked in a deep breath. 'They're good cops. The best.'

Rakesh gave his agreement in the form of a nod, but he didn't really agree. They were average cops who did what anyone would do, whether they were a seasoned detective, a senior officer or a beat cop. 'Weird thing, sir. I called Phoebe's phone and—'

'You *called* her phone? *Why?*'

'In case it was a mugging, sir. In case they'd taken it.' Rakesh pointed inside the shop. 'But it was sitting by the counter, face down.'

Asher took a few seconds to think it through. His brow knotted further with each one that passed. 'You think it was her husband, right?'

'That'd be my assumption, yes. Trouble is, he's not answering his phone.'

'Rakesh! You called *him* too?'

'Of course. He's our main suspect, right?'

'I guess so.'

'Helen's trying to track down his brother.' Rakesh looked over at her – whatever skills she had, tying up tape in the wind wasn't one of them. 'He's supposed to be staying with him.'

'Good. Finding him is your number one priority, okay?'

'Okay.' Rakesh nodded. 'Of course, sir.'

'Surely he'd take the phone, though?'

'That's my thinking, sir. But we're looking at this with rational brains. He's just smashed her head in with a lamp, so he's not rational... He's never killed before, so it's entirely possible he's panicked and fled, leaving it behind.'

'I see your point.' Asher ran his hand across his thinning scalp. 'I've requested the Edinburgh MIT are brought in, because we sure as hell can't manage a murder.' He gave a cold laugh. 'Just because it's only *attempted* murder doesn't change much, does it?'

'No, sir.'

The paramedics wheeled Phoebe out of the shop, accompanied by Bell, a look of grave concern on his face. They loaded her up into the ambulance with expert efficiency, then one hopped down and got behind the wheel.

Bell walked over to them just as the ambulance gave a squawk of siren – not that it needed it at this time, especially as most of the neighbours were outside watching events unfold. His gaze followed it leaving the scene, then shifted over to them. 'She's stable, sir, but struggling. They're taking her to the Royal Infirmary.'

'Thank you, George.' Asher clapped his back. 'Sounds like you saved her?'

Bell looked away. 'It was mostly Helen, sir.'

Asher laughed. 'Humble as well as handsome.'

Bell blushed. 'Me and Hel just about kept her going, but now it's down to the professionals.'

Asher clapped his hands together. 'Right. We need to get to the bottom of this, otherwise my arse is on the line here.' He focused on Bell, then Rakesh. 'Do we know who called it in?'

Rakesh pointed down the street to a man in his sixties in a fluorescent yellow running jacket, talking to Helen and Ella. 'Gentleman named Colin Stanton. Said he was up during the night for a pee. Got prostate troubles, as is pretty common for a man his age. Heard the window smash and came out. Saw it. Called it in.'

'Did he—'

'Didn't see who did it, no.'

Asher glanced at the shop again. 'Do we know if anything's missing?'

'A few lamps, possibly.' Bell thumbed over his shoulder. 'Cash box is lying on the floor. Looks like it's been broken into. Don't imagine there's ever a lot of cash in it, but still. And there are loads of business papers strewn about all over the office.'

Asher nodded slowly.

Rakesh glanced back at the shop. 'Are you assuming it's Lennon?'

'Tell me it's not, Sergeant. Prove it's not.'

Rakesh looked away from him.

'Okay, Sergeant, I want everyone in this street with a doorbell or security camera spoken to. Anyone who can't sleep and who looks out of their window in the middle of the night. And I want...' Asher trailed off.

Another car pulled up. A big American truck thing that would be more at home on a cattle ranch than in suburban Edinburgh.

The driver door opened and Marshall got out. He

looked around, then walked over to them with a friendly wave. 'Alright, Hamish.'

'Rob.' Asher frowned. 'What are you doing here?'

'Guess who has two thumbs and has just been allocated SIO to this murder case.' Marshall pointed both at himself. 'This guy.'

Asher raised his eyebrows, not exactly enjoying the joke. '*You* have? But you're based in the Borders?'

'I know.' Marshall pursed his lips. 'Me stupidly logging my location with Control when I was coming to speak to Rakesh was a schoolboy error.' He stood between Asher and Rakesh, as if he was blocking him off. 'The Edinburgh MIT will be taking it over in the morning and they're sending some bodies over now. Trouble is, they're already tied up with that decapitation on Princess Street.'

Bell gasped. '*Decapitation?*'

Marshall nodded. 'Don't know too much of the details, but word is someone's grandfather brought back a katana from Japan during the war. Anyway, they're busy and they need someone in charge. Hence me.'

'And you just so happened to be nearby.' Asher puffed his lips together. 'Meaning you're a DCI in an MIT, so why not use you until Edinburgh MIT gets their shite together?'

'Precisely.' Marshall nodded. 'Something like that, but it was put a bit less colourfully by DCS Potter.'

Only Rakesh flinched.

Maybe the nickname for her hadn't spread this far, or this low in the ranks.

Rakesh smiled at Marshall. 'Good news, Rob – it's not a murder.'

Marshall smiled at that. 'Ah. Interesting. Still, the same rules apply. We bring in forensics, we speak to people, we lock down the area.' He focused on Asher. 'Little birdie tells me you lot had her in for a domestic this evening?'

'Recipient of some abuse, aye.' Asher gave Rakesh a crafty glance. 'Husband was shouting, threatening to kill her in front of a few officers. We let him leave under investigative review.'

'Reasonable conclusion, sad outcome.' Marshall ran his hand down his face. 'Anyway, that's not on you or your team, but I guess we're all thinking it's likely he's returned to finish the job.' He looked at Rakesh. 'Obviously, you need to hunt for the victim's husband.'

# CHAPTER NINETEEN

The patrol car might have been a bit buggered but there was nothing wrong with the heating. He reached over to turn the heating down, but it already was. Great. Another thing to add to the long list of embuggerments.

Rakesh felt like he was going to fall asleep. His eyes kept misting over and shutting, blurring the road ahead. He wound down the window to let the ice-cold air in.

A fox darted across in front of him.

He braked hard and pulled to a stop.

It scuttled off and scurried under a fence.

Rakesh ran his hand down his face. He needed a cup of tea. Or a coffee. A very strong one.

When he worked down in the Borders, he didn't see a single fox in over a year. Now he was back in Edinburgh, he saw one a week.

He set off and took a right turn into a residential street, then felt the tug of sleep again. He couldn't stifle the yawn, as much as he tried and even with the window open. A stiff left turn onto an old council development – concrete houses built a little too close to the road and to each other.

And the other patrol car.

Rakesh pulled up behind Ella and Helen's vehicle on a quiet residential street, then grabbed his cap and got out into the freezing night. At least it had stopped raining. The pavement seemed dry enough to not be a minefield of black ice, but if Rakesh was anything, it was wary of ice, so he took it very slowly walking up to the drive outside the address, bracing himself on a buggered old camper van in the neighbour's drive.

'Bloody freezing.' Ella put her cap on. 'Helen's on a call with Wilson.'

Rakesh looked around the street. 'Do you know which—'

'Sarge, you worked for the rat sq— for the Complaints, didn't you?'

'I did.'

'If you don't mind me asking, how did you get into the Complaints?'

'I was a detective in the Borders MIT. Standard DS role. A case came up that had a tangent I was allowed to run with. Ended up arresting a couple of bent cops.'

'This was down in the Borders?'

'I was, but the corrupt cops were based in Edinburgh. Detectives, too. And the super in the Complaints liked what I did. How I worked the case and the results I got. I had a pretty good conviction rate.'

'This was the super who retired?'

'No. He wasn't there at the time. But he liked my work even more, hence me ending up working directly for him. We did some good stuff together. Some less so.' Rakesh smiled at her. 'Are you thinking of applying when you're a sergeant?'

'God no. But now you're here, working with us plebs.'

'And now I'm here.'

'Is this a demotion?'

'No. I'm at the same rank. Trouble is, I was a direct entry to detective sergeant. Pretty much the last one. Everyone hates us, because we haven't paid our dues. So it's been deemed that I need to serve my time in the trenches, as it were. And to pay my dues.'

'That seems like it sucks?'

'It doesn't suck, so much as...' Rakesh laughed. 'You're right. It sucks a bit.'

Ella grinned. 'We're not that bad, are we?'

'No. You're not. Helen's not. The rest of the team are fine.'

'And George?'

'George is George.'

'Aye, that's the truth...' Her eyes twitched, but she didn't seem to want to press it any further. 'Let's see if he's here.' She walked up the drive and rang the doorbell.

Rakesh shone his torch into the camper van. Powder blue sofa that probably folded out to provide a bed, but was presently stowed away. No sign of Lennon in there, but he wasn't fully satisfied – one of those old models that had more hidden nooks and crannies than an old Scottish castle.

The house door opened.

'Can I help you?'

Rakesh put his torch away and turned back around to the house.

A man looked out, shrouded by light. Tired, yawning. No mistaking him as being anyone other than Lennon's brother – he had the same everything. As bald and older – maybe forty – but he dressed like a stoned teenage gamer. The text on his turquoise T-shirt was an illegible shade of blue.

Ella gave a standard-issue polite glare. 'Looking for Dylan Blackwell.'

He gave a flash of his eyebrows. 'You've found him, sweetheart.'

Her glare turned into a smile, but lost much of its politeness. 'Gather Lennon Blackwell is your brother?'

Dylan looked away and puffed up his cheeks. 'Sadly, aye. Few years younger than me, but doesn't look it.' He glanced back at her, then did the up and down. 'Our mum had a bit of a thing for sixties songwriters.'

Rakesh laughed.

Ella frowned. 'What?'

'What do you mean?' Dylan scowled at her. 'Bob Dylan and John Lennon.'

Ella shrugged. 'Never heard of them.'

'My God...' Dylan's eyes went wide. 'Talk about police officers getting younger, eh?'

Ella folded her arms. 'Have you seen your brother tonight?'

'I did, aye.' Dylan exhaled slowly. 'Lennon called me earlier. In a bit of a state. Wanting into my house.'

'In a state?' Ella left a pause. 'Was he drunk?'

'God, no. *Upset*. Haven't seen him like that since Dad died.'

'Did he say why?'

'My brother's a bit of a closed book on that score.'

'But you saw him?'

'Right.'

Ella gestured behind Dylan. 'Is he here now?'

'No.'

'But he was here?'

'Right. I was out when he called. Had to cut my shift short.'

'Your shift?'

Dylan sighed. 'I'm a teacher. Have to work as a cabbie during the night to make ends meet.'

'Sorry to hear that. What do you teach?'

'Geography.' Dylan brushed a hand up his cheek. 'It is

what it is. Got an expensive divorce behind me, right? All I can do to hold on to this place.' He gestured at the house. 'Not much, I know, but it's mine and mine alone. And I want to keep it that way. Owning a place in Edinburgh's so bloody expensive now. Even here.'

'Were you driving your cab when he called?'

Dylan pointed behind them at a navy Tesla parked in a bay. Looked freshly cleaned, gleaming under the streetlights, a charging cable clawing its way over to attach like a parasite. 'Bought it with the old man's inheritance. Brother got a house, I got cash...' He sighed. 'Finished my shift early so I could come to let him in.'

Ella frowned. 'Hang on. You didn't collect him from the police station?'

'No. Told me he flagged down a cab and came here. I let him in and tried to calm him down. He told me you lot said he's to stay here for a couple of weeks?'

'He's been ordered to stay away from his wife.'

Dylan arched an eyebrow. 'With you now.'

'Did he say why?'

Dylan shook his head. 'Just that something happened between them.'

'Do you know where he is now?'

'He went for a walk. Hasn't returned. Bit annoying, to be honest you with you. I could've gone back on my shift and earned a few more quid. God knows I need it. I mean, *I* didn't inherit Dad's place, did I? As much of a bomb site as it was, it's worth a packet.'

Ella gave a kind smile. 'I take it you wouldn't mind us confirming that he's not here?'

'You want to check? Be my guest.' Dylan stepped aside and grimaced. 'I'm warning you, it needs a wee bit of a clean.'

Rakesh entered and quickly saw that Dylan was right to warn them. 'A wee bit of a clean' didn't do it justice – even a deep clean wouldn't have touched the surface.

No other way to put it – the place was a shit tip.

It needed a deep clean by a professional. And before that, a whole roll of black bin bags to get rid of the crap sitting everywhere.

Nuking the site from orbit wasn't the worst idea.

Ella brushed past and rattled up the stairs. 'I'll check up here, Sarge.'

'Good.' Rakesh stepped over an empty TV box and entered the living room. The TV itself was mounted up near the ceiling – must've been a massive strain to watch anything on it at that angle. Not that it was easy to get a seat on the sofa – it was stacked high with pizza boxes and takeaway wrappers, just a single space there. Three remotes and a PlayStation controller rested on the arm. Next to it, an ancient armchair had a tall pile of empty Pepsi Max wrappers, enough for 120 cans, at least twenty of which were crushed and discarded on the battered coffee table, along with bits of post, all unopened.

Despite all that, there was nowhere for Lennon to hide in there.

Rakesh had to enter the kitchen side on, as five wooden brushes were stacked up against the door. For no apparent reason – they clearly hadn't been used.

Maybe Dylan had another nocturnal side-line as a witch, flying over a sleeping Edinburgh on one of them.

If anything, the kitchen was even worse than the living room. Soiled plates filled the sink and the counter surrounding it. Two bin bags lay on the floor, both open and torn at the sides. Flies were swarming everywhere, despite the time of year.

Two doors.

The first was a small cupboard which contained another three brooms.

What the hell?

Rakesh opened the other door and had to cover his mouth and nose.

The toilet was disgusting. The lid was open, the pan unflushed. At least Dylan had crapped in the bowl, rather than on the floor. Specks of pee splashed all over the lino.

Rakesh walked back out into the hall and looked up the stairs. 'Anything?'

Ella appeared at the top, shaking her head. She clumped down the stairs.

Rakesh smiled at Dylan. 'Thank you for letting us validate that, sir.'

'No problem. Sorry it's a bit messy.'

Rakesh wanted to take him to task, but what would that achieve? 'Let us know when your brother resurfaces.'

'Why?'

'It's important we speak to him.'

'What's happened?'

'I'm not at liberty to divulge that, sir.' Rakesh handed him a business card. 'Just call me if and when he gets in touch.'

Dylan stared at it for a few seconds. 'Is it to do with Phoebe?'

Rakesh stood up tall. 'Why would you ask that?'

'Just... He said he's not to go to his house. Had a bit of a ding-dong with her.'

'That how he described it?'

'Kind of, aye.'

'Kind of?'

'Well, aye. Said it was a wee bit of back and forth.' Dylan reached into his pocket, then handed a card of his own to Rakesh. 'Listen, I'll keep an eye out for him but if you need to speak to me, the number's right there.'

# CHAPTER TWENTY

Rakesh slowed as they approached the roundabout by the giant Asda at the Jewel, then took a left. He reached over and picked up the radio. 'Control, this is ECC15. Negative at the brother's house. Over.'

The radio clicked. 'Negative at brother's house. ECC units copy? Over.'

Helen: 'ECC18 receiving. Copy. Over.'

Bell: 'ECC17 receiving. Copy. Over.'

Rakesh put the radio back to his mouth. 'Where are you both? Over.'

'Driving through deepest, darkest Niddrie just now, Sarge.' Bell left a lengthy pause. 'Can hear the twanging of banjos and the squealing of pigs.' Another pause, even longer. 'No sign of Lennon Blackwell, mind. Going to head back to their home, then start canvassing neighbours. Over.'

'Noted. Helen? Over.'

'I can hear the banjos twanging too. But not the pigs.' Her pause was frustratingly long and empty. 'Been speaking to this brother's taxi firm. His story checks out. PC Hale and I have been searching the area around Dylan's home. Nothing yet. This feels futile, Sarge. Over.'

Rakesh looked around at the college campus on the right. 'Report back in ten minutes. Over and out.' He put the radio back, then drove back along Milton Road towards the street Dylan lived on.

Talk about completing a circuit...

He sat back in his seat but didn't want to get too comfortable in the roasting heat. Even the sharp slap of the cold night air blasting in from the door hadn't woken him up. He still hadn't managed to get that cup of tea.

His phone rang. He got it out and looked at the display.

*Rob Marshall calling...*

Rakesh leaned forward and cleared his throat. He answered the call and put the phone to his ear. 'Hi, Rob. What's up?'

'How's it going?'

'All my PCs are out. Well, the ones I've got who aren't looking for Dawn O'Keefe.'

The line went silent.

Rakesh had to pull the phone away from his ear to check Marshall was still on the call.

'Dawn? Ah, missing teenager. Got it. No sign of Lennon?'

'Nope. But I didn't expect one so easily. And driving around in cars with glowing signs reading POLICE in English and Gaelic isn't the most subtle way to play it.'

Marshall laughed down the line.

'Feels futile, Rob.'

'Aye, and that'll be because police work like that mostly is, Rakesh. It feels futile, because it is futile. 99.9999% chance he's not going to be walking around this area, right? But that 0.0001% chance means if we don't...' Marshall sighed. 'You know how you don't find him here? You don't look.'

'Got it.'

'I appreciate this is your first stint in uniform, Rakesh. I had a year of it in the Met. I knew I was to become an inspector, but they put me in as a constable first. Eight months of that, just walking the beat in Wembley, Brentford and Chelsea. Then four months as a uniform sergeant in Brick Lane. Then I moved over to detective as an inspector. I felt like I lost an IQ point with each shift.'

Rakesh didn't know what to say to that. Uniformed officers were much maligned in the MIT, but the ones he'd worked with were just as smart as any detectives and would've made good ones had they chose to shift over. 'I miss the work.'

'Yeah, that'd get at me. Listen, I've got a job for you, Rakesh.'

Rakesh leaned forward, excitement bubbling in his stomach. 'What is it?'

'Need you to notify Phoebe's next of kin.'

Rakesh sat back, the bubbles popping and disappearing. 'Okay.'

'Don't be like that, Rakesh. It's very much a sergeant's job.'

'That'll be her sister, right?'

'I guess so. Brief her, then get one of your constables to drive her to the hospital.'

# CHAPTER TWENTY-ONE

'I grew up here.' Ella pointed at the end of the street. Over a tall brick wall, an old kiln glowed under heavy spotlights. An ancient thing, long out of use, but it probably made several of the bricks used to build the nearby houses. She looked around the quiet street, rammed with parked cars. 'Kind of miss the place, you know?'

Rakesh didn't really – he hated where he'd grown up and only briefly returned to see his parents. The cold wind here made Rakesh wake up a bit. In the distance, the waves crashed on the beach. The only other times he'd been to Porty, the sea had been far out, miles away from the shore. Felt like he'd imagined it – maybe he should bring Afri here tomorrow for a walk. She'd enjoy it, maybe get lunch in that nice-looking pub around the corner. 'Where do you live now?'

'Gorgie. Not a fan. Anything past the end of Princes Street feels like Glasgow.'

'Nothing wrong with Glasgow.'

'Sure, but it's not Edinburgh, is it?'

'True.' Whatever that meant...

Helen was in their car, talking on the radio.

A shiver crawled up Rakesh's spine. 'After this, we're going to McDonald's for coffee.'

'Oh, Sarge, McDonald's? Pushing the boat out, eh? A special occasion?'

Rakesh laughed. 'No, it's just the only place that's open at this time.' He walked over to the tenement door, buffeted by the wind, and pressed the buzzer. 'Bloody hell, that's fresh.'

'You get used to it, Sarge. Living on the North Sea.'

'Isn't that the Forth?'

'Aye, but it's the same difference.' Ella looked around, yawning. 'Really could do with a coffee, now you mention—'

'WHO THE FUCK ARE YOU?' The distorted female voice leapt out of the intercom speaker like a punch in the kidneys.

Rakesh stepped forward. 'Police.' He gave her a few seconds. 'We need—'

'Will you quit jabbing my buzzer, you fu—'

'My name is Sergeant Rakesh Siyal. We're looking for Jennifer Sheridan.'

The intercom crackled.

'That's me.' Jennifer sniffed. 'What's this about?'

'We need a word.'

'At one in the bloody morning? Are you off your head?'

'It's about your sister.'

'Phoebe? What's happened?'

'Please, we really should do this inside.'

A long pause.

A rasping sigh.

'Fine.'

The buzzer sounded and the door lock clicked.

Rakesh went first, leading Ella along a hallway, then up two flights of stairs to an area exposed to the biting wind. A door on the left for flat 6, then a platform leading along to another door, hanging ajar. He nudged it fully open – it didn't lead into a flat, but another hallway with two front doors. The one on the left was open, though, so he entered. 'Jennifer?'

'I'm here.' She stood in a tight hallway, arms folded, looking all ruffled, like they'd woken her from a deep sleep. Pink pyjama bottoms and a green jumper with HUFFLEPUFF screaming out. Monster claw slippers. 'What's happened?'

'We're sorry to report that there was a break-in at your shop and—'

'Is she okay?'

'Your sister's in hospital.'

'But you're not saying she's well, are you?'

'We need—'

'You need me to go to the hospital, don't you?'

Rakesh frowned, sensing her seeming refusal to be at her ailing sister's side. Could be because it was the middle of the night, but her snarl made Rakesh wonder if there was something else. Something deeper. Or maybe something shallower. 'Unless there's another next of kin who could—?'

'Obviously there's her husband, but...' She snorted. 'He's not exactly on your Christmas card list, is he?'

'What about your folks?'

'They're halfway to the Azores just now, so they won't be much use.' Jennifer walked through an immaculate living room with a designer sofa and several lamps that probably came from the shop, into a narrow kitchen. She stood there, staring into space, hand resting on the antique kettle on the hob. She looked over at them in the doorway. 'We were going to go away on holiday over Christmas while the shop's shut. Just me and Pheebs. Because our folks will be in Chile. First time we'd not all spend it together in our lives.' She looked over at Rakesh with a frown. 'Will she be able to go?'

'I'm unsure on that just now.' Rakesh looked out of the kitchen window and saw Helen still in the patrol car down below. He turned back and gestured toward Ella. 'My colleague here will drive you to the hospital and the doctors there will be able to advise you.'

Jennifer looked over at Ella, then back to Rakesh. 'Do I *have* to go?'

Ella stepped closer to her. 'I don't think you quite understand the magnitude of this.'

Jennifer furrowed her brow. 'Listen, I love my sister, but I'm not a doctor, am I? So what good can I do? I'd rather head to the shop.'

'You mean, go to work?'

'Aye. We've got a big sale starting tomorrow. Need to see the state of the place.' She checked her watch. 'It's already tomorrow. They'll be queuing outside the shop at ten, you mark my words.'

Rakesh couldn't believe it. He thought he'd seen everything, but this... Wow. 'Ms Sheridan, it's important we take you to see your sister.'

'Fine.' Jennifer sighed. 'Right. You win.' She rubbed at her forehead. 'I better get changed, hadn't I?' She grabbed a pile of clothes hanging on the back of a kitchen chair, then pulled off her jumper, so she was standing there topless.

Not the first time Rakesh had seen that – to some, the police weren't people, so they could do the strangest things in your presence...

Or they'd do it to see if you're watching and then complain about you.

Or just for the sheer thrill of it.

Before he could turn away, she slipped off her pyjama bottoms now and stood there naked except for socks. 'Will you give me a lift back home afterwards?'

Rakesh turned to look out of the window.

He could still see her reflection as she pulled on her bra.

So he looked up at the ceiling. In the corner, a spider was all coiled up, waiting for spring. 'I'm afraid we can't provide a return lift.'

'Bloody typical.'

Ella was blushing. 'When did you last see her?'

'This evening. At the shop. '

'When?'

'Just before ten?'

Ella frowned. 'Phoebe owns it, right?'

'We both do. Dad transferred it to us when he retired.' Rakesh caught Jennifer pulling up her jeans in the window. 'I'm not really good at running the place, so Pheebs does all the business side. I'm shit hot at selling lights to people, though. Dad said I have the gift of the gab, which means I'm a gobshite. So it works well for both of us.'

'And you saw her this evening?'

'Right.' Jennifer hauled on her top and Rakesh could look directly at her again, tugging her hair down with her fingers. 'I tried to do a lot of the prep for the sale tonight, but Pheebs wanted to finesse it. So I left.'

Ella nodded slowly. 'Did she tell you what happened with Lennon?'

'She said they'd had cross words.' Jennifer laughed bitterly as she hauled on her socks. 'I mean, threatening to kill someone isn't "having words", is it? She said she was going to come here after she finished. I've got a spare bed all made up for her. But she didn't show.'

'You didn't wait up for her?'

'I told her to be half an hour at most, but... She's strong willed.' Jennifer shrugged. 'She's got a key. Used it to let herself in earlier. It's not just for watering plants when I'm away... Or feeding this monster.' A cat jumped up onto the table and rubbed its face against Jennifer. She ran a hand down the length of its back, then looked over at them. 'It wasn't the first time she's stayed here after an argument with him.'

Ella raised an eyebrow. 'Oh?'

'Just a bit tempestuous, that's all.' Jennifer slipped on the other sock. 'Never came to blows or anything...'

'Do you get on well with Lennon?'

'Kind of. Most of the time, he's lovely. Kind, smart, funny. But see when he gets a drink in him... And I don't mean a skinful. Any amount of booze. Like just one pint. And he just goes nuts.'

'What do you mean by nuts?'

'Constantly thinks she's sleeping around. And she isn't. Of course she isn't. She loves him. But he's so insecure.' Jennifer tickled the cat, eliciting a deep purr. 'I know him really well. Lennon's brother, Dylan... We, uh, dated for a few months. We hooked up at their wedding a few years back. Both got really, really wasted and... He'd just broken up with his ex. Daft idea. I knew we'd be a disaster. And we were.'

'Why was that daft?'

'He's a Capricorn. I'm a Leo.'

Ella scowled at her. 'Sorry, why does that—'

'Trust me.' Jennifer raised a hand. 'Dyl's a typical Capricorn. Blunt to the point of rude. And so persistent. And so, *so* needy.'

'I don't know why that means you know why Lennon is insecure, though?'

'Eh? Lenny's birthday is eight days after Dyl's. He's four years younger, mind, but he's still a Capricorn. They're both so needy. So typical in them.'

Rakesh tried to swallow down the words, to stop them coming out. 'We need to track down your sister's husband.'

'So you think he did something to her?' Jennifer held up a hand again. 'Of course you do. He threatens her, then someone attacks her. Doesn't take a genius to figure that one out.'

Rakesh nodded. 'Do you have any idea where he could go?'

Jennifer took a look around the room, then shrugged. 'Dylan's?' She frowned. 'But they fell out over something. Heard all about it from Pheebs.'

'So they were estranged?'

'This was a while ago, so maybe they've patched things up.'

'Do you know what happened?'

'It was about putting their mum into a home. Dylan

wanted to look after her. Lennon didn't want to waste the money on paying for a care home. She was living at home, but... It got messy. Leaving the house in the middle of the night, completely naked, and trying to get on a night bus. Putting out the neighbours' bins on a Saturday, naked. That was the last straw. She's in a home now, which is good for all of them. Weird family, I have to say.'

'How do you mean?'

'Dyl's parents split when they were young. They're half-brothers. Same mum. Both dads are dead, but Lennon ended up inheriting *his* dad's place. Dyl's old man died with, like, seventeen credit cards all maxed out, but he got something from Lennon's dad. The house went to Lennon. And Dyl insisted they keep their mum's place and not pay for a care home. He was looking after her and it didn't go well. Think it all got too much for him.'

Rakesh stood there, thinking it all through.

That maybe explained the sheer state of his house. Not only was he having to do two jobs to keep his head above water on his mortgage, but he'd been looking after their mother – all to inherit a house rather than have it swallowed up by care bills.

But it also opened other doors, giving more possibilities for intrigue. A half-brother potentially aggrieved by his sibling's good fortune.

And of course, Rakesh had to remember he wasn't a detective anymore, like everyone kept telling him. He was a uniform sergeant, so he gestured to the side. 'My colleague here will take you to see Phoebe.'

Jennifer swallowed. 'Sure thing.'

Rakesh followed her out of the kitchen. Then something hit him. 'Jennifer, do you know which theatre Lennon worked at?'

# CHAPTER TWENTY-TWO

Rakesh parked outside the Burke and Hare Theatre on Grindlay Street behind another squad car. He took a last glug of his McDonald's coffee, and swallowed it right down. That place had no right to make such nice coffee. And to think, he didn't used to drink anything with caffeine in. Now he was up to four cups a day.

He got out into a surprisingly warm night – central Edinburgh was much warmer than out in Portobello. Or maybe the coffee was just hitting the spot, at least heat-wise.

Bell got out of the other car. 'Sarge.'

'Thanks for joining me.'

'So much for frontline police, eh? Great night to rob a house in Niddrie.' Bell paused, waiting for his terrible joke to hit. It didn't. 'Like there's anything worth nicking.'

Rakesh ignored it and instead walked up to the theatre door.

The front of the building was covered in arty posters for edgy productions: *Hamlet* starring a trans man; *The Picture of Dorian Gray* where everyone was gender-swapped; *Othello* with a Scottish Asian cast; a musical about the Declaration of Arbroath in the style of *Hamilton*.

Six posters advertised the forthcoming production of *MacBeth MSP*, set in the Scottish Parliament. The lead actor was someone off the telly.

Rakesh shone his torch in through the window. One of those modern spaces that was all concrete and steel. More posters of further plays. *The Lost Laddie from Orkney*, featuring a ginger kid at a piano. *Bloody Idiot*, a *Trainspotting* knock-off about a football hooligan. *Ghost in the Machine*, a haunted detective doing haunted detective things in Edinburgh.

No signs of anyone inside, though.

Rakesh swung the torch further over and caught the large metal doors leading into the auditorium. 'Not sure why I was expecting anyone to be here...' He looked back at Bell.

Another squad car pulled up.

Helen got out and walked over to join them, followed by Ella. 'Jennifer's at the hospital now, Sarge.'

'Thanks.' Rakesh handed them the tray with two coffees. 'Here you go.'

'Cheers, Sarge.'

'Which is— Oh, got it.'

Bell finished his own coffee, then pointed at the theatre, the sign caught in a pale purple light. 'What a name, eh?' He shook his head. 'Who calls a theatre after Edinburgh's worst serial killers?'

Helen shrugged. 'Or the lap-dancing bar around the corner.'

Bell laughed. 'Oh, aye. Forgot about that. Awful place.'

Helen raised her eyebrows. 'Used to dance there when I was eighteen.'

Bell's eyes bulged. '*You* did?'

'Easy pocket money.' Helen smiled and looked back the way. 'Ah, sweet memories.' Then she rolled her eyes at him. 'Of course I didn't. Jesus. Who do you think I am, George?'

'No comment.' Bell was blushing as he walked over to the door and shook the handle. He started stroking his chin. 'Where could he be, eh?'

'Hey, do you know something?' Helen joined him by the door. 'Lennon Blackwell works here. And there's a light on inside.'

Bell nodded and gave the kind of theatrical wink Rakesh expected to see on the stage. 'Lennon has a key, so we really should clear the place because he might be here.' He looked at Rakesh with all the ham of the worst actor who trod the boards in that place. 'Right, Sarge?'

Rakesh stood tall. 'We can't break in.'

Bell pursed his lips. 'Sure. Of course we can't.' Another crafty wink.

'I mean it. We don't have a warrant.'

'Aye, aye.' Bell crouched to check the lock, but he used his torso to block it from Rakesh. He stood back up and opened the door. 'Would you look at that? Someone left the door open for us.' He winked as he pocketed the knife he'd used to prise open the lock, then gestured inside. 'You first, Sarge.'

Rakesh sighed. 'I guess we need to check and see if someone broke in.' He turned to Helen and Ella. 'Helen, you guard this door. Ella, can you find any other exits while we search?' He led Bell through, then shone his torch around, getting a better view now he was inside.

Bell walked over and reached for the lights.

Rakesh whispered, 'No.'

'See your point.' Bell hopped up and over the partition to the box office, then disappeared below it. Seconds later, his head bobbed up again. 'Clear, Sarge.'

Rakesh took his time assessing the location.

The door burst open and Ella walked out of the unisex toilets, shaking her head. 'All of the stalls are empty, Sarge.'

Bell stood by the door to the auditorium, torch off, eyebrow raised.

Rakesh joined him and stood there, listening long enough to hear it was silent.

Soft footsteps as Ella continued off along the corridor.

'Sod it.' Bell heaved open the hulking left door and stepped into the auditorium.

'Careful...' Rakesh scanned his torch around the giant grey concrete box. Rows and rows of rock-hard concrete benches – the kind you'd find in the average jail cell – were softened by cushions and throws. His tiptoed footsteps were like cannonball shots – the place must be murder when someone walked off for a mid-show pee.

Bell walked up to the stage. The curtains hung open, showing a pretty good replica of the Scottish Parliament's main chamber like it was in the middle of First Minster's Questions. Nobody was there, save for the mannequins masquerading as the cabinet.

Maybe using dummies was an upgrade from the real thing...

Rakesh walked further into the room, closer to Bell, then he swung around to look behind them. Above the entrance, the sound desk loomed in darkness.

If Lennon was anywhere...

Rakesh swept his torch around the walls and found a door marked STAFF ONLY.

'Come on.' Rakesh led Bell through to the technical area, all bare pipes and rougher concrete blocks. A staircase of bare metal steps, presumably leading up to the sound desk. He set a foot on the staircase and it resonated through his whole body.

*Spectacular...*

He took it very slowly climbing the stairs, but felt like

he was riding a charging elephant while beating two bin lids together.

A huge window looked out onto the stage. Before it, a giant sound desk filled most of the area, hundreds of knobs and dials and faders spreading across, sandwiched between floor-standing speakers and smaller ones that looked even more expensive.

Rakesh walked over to it. Over to the side was another desk, more humble and presumably the lighting desk. Everything was meticulously marked up with tape of all colours, each one scribbled upon.

> FRONT LEFT
> FRONT RIGHT
> REAR SPOTS
> MACBETH SPOT

Lennon Blackwell's domain.

Rakesh swept his torch across the surface but didn't see anything on it that could lead them to his location.

Wait.

Something was underneath.

'Sarge, are—'

He raised a hand to cut off Bell, then flicked his torch to a wider beam and lit up the underneath of the desk.

A sleeping bag.

And someone was in it.

Either a homeless person or...

He twisted his torch to narrow the beam – and confirmed it was Lennon Blackwell.

Bell caught his nod and rounded the desk, drawing his baton.

Rakesh stepped back and pulled his taser out of the holster, then painted Lennon with the red laser sights. He counted on his fingers.

Three.

Two.

One.

Bell reached over and tapped him.

Lennon opened his eyes. He lashed out with a foot and sent Bell flying.

Bell tumbled over, cracking his hip off the floor.

There it was – active resistance.

Rakesh pulled the trigger.

The end of the taser just sparked.

Bell glowered up at him. 'Did you replace the cartridge?'

*Shite.*

Lennon got up, but his sleeping bag caught around his knees.

Rakesh grabbed hold of his arms.

Lennon jerked forward and Rakesh slipped, dropping the taser.

Lennon used the temporary advantage to push Rakesh back against the lighting rig, making him sprawl all over it.

The auditorium below lit up like the surface of the sun.

Bell was on his feet now, swinging his baton towards Lennon.

Lennon kicked the sleeping bag into his face, then grabbed a microphone and smashed it into Bell's nose.

Bell screamed out and sank to his knees, covering his face with his hands.

Rakesh lashed out with his baton, but Lennon dodged him. Rakesh swung hard and missed, making him tumble forward. He braced himself against the sound desk, then turned around.

Lennon chucked a sandbag towards him.

It caught Rakesh in the stomach.

The wind rushed out of him and he cracked his head against the wall.

Footsteps raced away from him as he slid down.

Rakesh could only sit there, his midriff burning. He sucked in a deep breath and started to feel something back in his guts.

Bloody hell.

Bell walked over and reached out a hand to help Rakesh up. 'Come on, Sarge. No time for that sort of thing.'

Rakesh grabbed it, then stood up again. He sucked in a deep breath, followed him over the floor, then raced back down the staircase back into the bright auditorium.

No sign of Lennon down here.

He walked through to the entrance.

Helen stood there, arms folded. Bored. 'What's up with you pair?'

Rakesh stopped, his breath short. 'Did he come this way?'

'Would I be standing here if he did?'

'Has Ella found the other entrance?'

'Nope. She saw the light show inside and went to investigate. Thought it was you two fannying about.'

'Stay here.' Rakesh ran back inside.

Bell was in the glowing main theatre with the lights on full.

So bright Rakesh had to cover his eyes with a hand.

Ella lay on the floor, cradling her head. 'Caught me from behind.'

The curtain ruffled on the stage, half open at the side.

'That was shut earlier.' Bell ran over and vaulted up onto the stage, then disappeared through the curtains.

Rakesh helped Ella to her feet. 'Go to Helen and check the front.'

'Sarge.'

Rakesh raced over to the stage, but struggled to get up there. Took him three goes, but he finally managed it.

Bell was at the back of the theatre, standing next to an open door. 'Sarge!' He disappeared outside.

Rakesh followed him, stepping out onto a square stuck between the tenements – you wouldn't know it was there. Parked cars hid in front of office buildings, still lit up like it was a working day but not as bright as the auditorium. He followed Bell along the path, then stopped alongside him on Bread Street.

They both swung around, looking in all directions.

The lane continued on up to East Fountainbridge.

Bread Street ran towards Lothian Road in one direction, with the other leading to the Castle and the Royal Mile, or onto the West Port and the Grassmarket.

Each junction spread out with further possibilities, further potential routes.

And they had no indication which one Lennon had taken.

Rakesh let out a sigh. 'Call it in.'

# CHAPTER TWENTY-THREE

The night had cooled a few degrees in mere minutes. And a thin rain started, misting the empty street. A wave of taxis passed over on Lothian Road, swooshing through the puddles.

Rakesh checked his phone, but still nothing from Marshall or Asher.

Bell walked out of the theatre and shook his head. 'Definitely not here, Sarge.'

Rakesh wiped rain out of his face. '*Definitely*?'

'Far as I can tell, aye.' Bell stepped in close. 'Need to remind you of that training directive about tasers, don't I?'

Rakesh blew out a deep breath. This wasn't a good look and if anyone was going to pay the price for letting their chief suspect go, it was going to be him. He'd watched that film many times before, just hadn't been the protagonist.

Bottom line was he hadn't replaced his taser cartridge after arresting Keegan, so it was his fault. All his fault.

Bell nudged his arm. 'Go back up there and pop off a spare cartridge.' He tapped his nose, then grunted. 'It'll be like you missed. I won't say a word, Sarge.'

'No, George. I made a mistake but I won't compound it by lying. I'll brief Inspector Asher on the matter.' Rakesh fixed a stare on Bell. 'Right now, I need you to check through Lennon's possessions inside and see if we can find any clues as to where he's been tonight.'

'On it, Sarge.' Bell slipped off back inside the theatre.

Rakesh let another deep breath go, but his guts were aching. Not just from being winded. Something else lingered around. Probably the sheer disappointment of the news from Marshall. Another four months of this. And he wasn't cut out for it.

Two cars pulled up along the road. One was a muscle truck, the other a squad car with a handbrake that didn't seem to be the most secure from the way it wobbled when Asher got out.

Asher looked around the vicinity. 'Are you all okay?'

'Ella and I were attacked, but we're both fine, sir.' Rakesh rubbed his neck. 'I'm sorry, sir. We lost him.' He maintained eye contact as he walked towards him – he had to face the punishment directly. 'We had him. Thought he was asleep. Then he attacked PC Bell. My taser was ineffective.'

'It happens. Reason I hate the things. It's not like a real gun where you take them down.'

'When I went to taser him, I'd forgotten to put a new cartridge on, so I just got sparks. And he got away.'

'Shit happens.' Asher sniffed. 'Good cops with honest hearts can make mistakes all day long without repercussion. Suggest you go back and pop off a spare cartridge, Rakesh.'

'I'd rather face—'

'Rakesh, you're not listening.' Asher raised his eyebrows. 'Check the location. It's possible you made a mistake.'

Rakesh hated this kind of nonsense. Minor levels of corruption. 'If you insist, sir.'

'I do. There's a good lad.' Asher nodded at Marshall as he arrived. 'Rob, I need you to get some detectives on this, immediately.'

'On it already.' Marshall folded his arms. 'Got a team going through the CCTV on Lothian Road.' He swung around. 'Trouble is, this is central Edinburgh so it's pretty far from my patch and totally different. Around here, you've got as many streets in a square mile as there are in the whole of a Borders town. He could've got up to the Royal Mile in five minutes, or down to Haymarket or to the New Town or up to the university. Could be hiding in any number of doorways.'

Asher nodded. 'Probably caught a cab.'

'I'll get people on that, see if anyone's prepared to

help.' Marshall's phone rang. He fished it out and checked the display. Then rubbed it free of rain. He stuck his tongue in his cheek. 'What do these idiots want?' He walked off, phone to his ear.

Asher watched him go. 'This isn't on us, Rakesh. We're short-staffed and doing our best in the circumstances.' He looked over at him. 'Just glad you're all okay.'

Another car rolled up, coming to a halt between two cones of light, rattled by the wind and rain.

Two shifty men got out and looked around. The bigger one walked over to them, grinning wide, but his eyes were narrowed. 'DI Dean Craven.' He thrust out a hand to Asher. 'Edinburgh drugs squad.'

The other one followed him over. A middle-aged, overweight Asian guy. He looked Rakesh up and down, then stood a bit too close. 'DCI Mike Mukherjee. Dean's boss.' He winked at Asher. 'And your worst nightmare.'

Asher laughed. 'In my nightmares, I'm naked and back at school with a puddle of urine at my feet. That your thing, champ?'

Mukherjee looked around, clicking his tongue. 'What's going on here?'

Marshall walked back over and got between them. 'Okay, lads. Back off a bit, eh?'

Craven ran a hand down Marshall's arm, like a lover would. A cheeky glint filled his eyes. 'I'd say it's nice to meet you, Rob, but we already did. A few months ago, if you remember?'

'Oh, I remember. You tried to pass the buck then, guess you're going to try to do the same here.' Marshall folded his arms. 'As I just told you on the phone, I'm the SIO on this case. Temporarily. I'll ask you again, and this time I expect an answer – why are you here?'

Craven took his hand away from Marshall to point at the theatre. 'Because this location is under surveillance as part of a drug investigation.'

Marshall glowered at him. 'You're investigating Lennon Blackwell?'

'No, Dylan.'

Marshall frowned. 'His brother?'

'That's the one. You're smarter than you look.' Craven nodded. "What's your interest in him?'

Marshall laughed. 'Oh, Dean. You want me to show you mine first, don't you?'

'Have it your way. You'll just be disappointed.' Craven grinned and pretended to open his flies. 'Okay, so the story goes a little something like this. Like so many teachers, poor ickle Dylan has to drive a taxi at night as well as teach people's brats during the day. But in his case, we think that nocturnal activity is a cover for him dealing drugs.'

Marshall looked away, nodding. 'Explains a few things. Is he connected?'

'Nope. And that's the problem.'

'You mean you haven't arrested him because he's connected? Or you haven't arrested him because you get confused between which is your arse and which is your elbow?'

Craven leaned back and roared with laughter.

'Lads, lads, lads.' Mukherjee raised a hand. 'We don't want him arrested if we can avoid it. Dylan's small fry. We want to use him to climb up the chain. But *only* if he's connected to a chain.'

'Hang on, so you *don't* think he is?'

'We just don't know.' Mukherjee flared his nostrils. 'It's possible he's flying solo. Which is bad news, because it implies chaos. And chaos in the drug world is the only thing worse than the existence of the drug world.'

Marshall looked at Rakesh then back at Mukherjee. 'Struggling to see how this is my problem?'

Mukherjee laughed. 'It's your problem because you've stomped right into a location we believe contains a cache of drugs.' He waved a hand along the road. 'Dylan regularly picks up fares on this street. We think his brother might be storing the gear for him to deal to his passengers.'

'Fine, but that's nothing to do with my case.'

Craven picked something out of his teeth. 'Except for the fact I got called out of bed at eleven o'clock because Sheridan Lighting is also a flagged location.'

Mukherjee clamped a hand on Craven's arm. 'And when Dean gets woken up, he calls me. So I get woken up too. And I need my beauty sleep.'

'Looks like you're overdue for a nap, big man.'

Marshall narrowed his eyes. 'You think Phoebe Blackwell is involved in this?'

'No, but her sister is a known associate of Dylan. And it's possible Phoebe was attacked because of what Dylan's been doing.'

'Which is?'

Craven laughed. 'Are you deaf? Dealing drugs.'

Marshall fixed his smile on him. 'Lots of people deal drugs, Dean. Most of them don't get their sisters-in-law attacked.'

Craven looked into a puddle like he might find some sense there, then back up at Marshall. 'We have intel suggesting Dylan has been playing fast and loose with the jurisdictions of various Edinburgh drug gangs. We just don't know if he's operating for one of them.'

'Okay. She was attacked in the light shop. Whose area's that in?'

'Big Dunc's domain, that.'

'Big Dunc?'

'Duncan Hetherstone. Lives in Cupar, would you believe, but has a tight grip on Edinburgh.'

Marshall nodded. 'Glad it's not our mutual friend down in the Borders.'

'Oh, there's no love lost there.'

Marshall smiled. 'Do you think he was storing drugs in her light shop too?'

Mukherjee shook his head. 'Nope.'

'So why was it under surveillance?'

'Because we think he was using the shop to launder money.'

Marshall looked over at Rakesh – he'd seen that look before. Marshall didn't believe a word of it. He looked back to Mukherjee. 'Have you got any proof of that?'

'We've been working on it. We've got some forensic accountants going through the books and it doesn't stack up at all. Likewise, Dylan made an inordinately high number of trips to Duddingston.' Craven dug his pinkie nail into his teeth. 'I mean, I love the place. Very pretty wee village. Nice pub there. Lots of walks up Arthur's Seat. But hardly anyone lives there. So no need for anything like that volume of taxi journeys there.'

Rakesh waited for Mukherjee to look at him. 'I have a potential explanation.'

'Go on?'

'Her husband suspected Phoebe was having an affair.'

Mukherjee raised his eyebrows. 'With her brother-in-law? Now *that* is cheeky.'

'Never said that.'

'No. But you've thought it.'

Marshall raised a hand. 'Have you actually found any drugs?'

'Not yet. Just got intel to that effect. Good stuff too, enough for a warrant.'

Marshall smiled. 'For here?'

'Aye.' Mukherjee pointed inside the theatre. 'Now the cat's out of the bag, though, I've got a meat wagon on the way here full of thugs all desperate to claw away at every square inch of that place.'

'But you're telling me you have nothing?'

Craven sighed. 'We think his temporary stash is either here or the light shop.'

'And the bigger stash?'

'Their mum's place.' Mukherjee pulled his phone out of his pocket. 'Old dear got put in a home recently, so there's nobody at the house. And before that, she wasn't in a good way. Meanwhile, Dylan was there every day. Enough to let us get a search warrant. We were planning to start by the dawn's early light.' He pointed at Craven. 'Then this attempted murder got called in and we needed to change tack.'

'So we decided to take a wait-and-see approach.' Craven shoved his phone back in his pockets. 'And now we've waited and seen.'

# CHAPTER TWENTY-FOUR

Rakesh stood in the middle of his team. Or what remained of them. Bell, Helen and Ella spread out across the front of the place, establishing a perimeter while the drugs and MIT detectives conducted a search inside an address.

Prestonfield Road was a typical post-war Edinburgh street, narrowed by parked cars. The row of double-parked patrol cars thickened the artery even further. Sitting in the shadow of Arthur's Seat, that bulbous leonine hill overlooking the city centre, but you'd never know at this time of night and in this downpour – the sky was a black and grey mess, the wind blowing the rain around chaotically.

Ella and Helen were at each end with Bell nearest him in the middle.

Nobody in or out without the explicit say-so of both

Marshall and Mukherjee.

Not that anyone had come anywhere near.

Bell sidled up to Rakesh. 'Perfect hideout, isn't it?'

'Have thought that.' Rakesh winced at another stab of pain in his guts. He waved around the place. 'Can you please move back, George?'

'Sure. But there's nobody running away from there, is there?' Bell walked back to his post. 'No bugger around...'

Cheeky sod.

Bell thought he knew everything about the job, when the reality was he was just another arrogant arsehole who'd coasted on attitude.

Another stab of pain even deeper in his guts made Rakesh look over at the house.

A single-storey post-war building, its attic conversion's dormers popping up through the red slates and making the place look like a frog with bulging eyes.

A door slammed behind him.

Rakesh swung around.

A man was walking away from a neighbouring house. Middle-aged, his dressing gown struggling to contain his bulk. Hairy feet stuffed into navy moccasins. He was heading right for Bell. 'What's going on here?'

Rakesh intercepted him. 'This is a police matter, sir.'

The neighbour looked him up and down. 'I can bloody see that. It's half one in the bloody morning! What are you playing at?'

'My name's Rakesh Siyal, sir. I'm a sergeant in Police

Scotland, based at Craigmillar station. I'm sorry, but this is a crucial police matter and—'

'Can't this wait?'

'No, sir, we need to—'

'Is this about that girl? Dawn or something?'

Rakesh gritted his teeth. 'I can't comment, sir.'

'You think she's been brought here? To Audrey's?'

'I said I—'

'I get it.' He shot Rakesh a crafty wink. 'Haven't seen the old girl in months, have to say.' He ran a hand through his thick hair. 'Bloody hell. Has some filthy nonce brought her here?'

Rakesh held his gaze, giving him absolutely nothing. 'Have you seen anyone in the vicinity this evening?'

'Well. There was some movement in there earlier, but... I didn't see anyone coming or going. Could've been nothing.'

'Was it either of her sons?'

'Are you saying Lennon and Dylan are... are paedophiles?'

'No, sir. I'm not. Have you seen them?'

'You think one of them has brought a child to *our* street?'

Rakesh held his gaze. He wasn't getting anywhere with him. 'Thank you, sir. We need you to give us space.'

'Sure you do.' The neighbour gave him another look up and down, then nodded slowly. 'You have my full and unwavering support, Sergeant. I hope you find her. And alive too.'

'Thank you, sir.'

The neighbour walked back to his house, but he stopped outside his front door without opening it. He turned to watch them, wanting to witness them rescuing a girl who wasn't even there. He looked across the street and cupped his hands around his mouth. 'It's about that missing lassie, Tony!'

A similarly dressed neighbour waved a hand. 'Dawn, isn't it?'

'Aye. He reckons some nonce has brought her here! To Audrey's!'

'Fuck's sake! One of her sons?'

'Don't know! But I always thought Dylan's a shifty bugger!'

'Same!' The other neighbour glowered. 'What's that going to do to our house prices?'

Rakesh winced, but he didn't want any more hassle from the neighbours, so he let them believe their fantasy. 'Thank you, gentlemen. We'll be in touch with you both if we need any further assistance.'

They both nodded, then went back inside their homes.

Now it was Helen's turn to break formation and walk over to Rakesh. 'Sure you should've let him think that?'

'I didn't let him think anything. He thought it all himself.' Rakesh caught a look from Bell, but ignored it. 'I just didn't disabuse him of that notion.'

'I see your point.' Helen frowned. 'Are you okay?'

'I'm fine. Why?'

'It's just you keep wincing.'

'Do I? Well, I'm fine.'

'You're not. What's up?'

'That Imodium isn't working.'

'So ask to go in there, then.'

Rakesh motioned with his hands for her to move away. 'Can you get back into formation?'

'It's not like...' Helen stopped and scuttled off back to her post.

Rakesh turned around and spotted Marshall walking back out of the house, shaking his head – they'd struck out. He walked over to him. 'Nothing?'

'Nothing.' Marshall got out his phone and checked the screen. 'Still early days, Rakesh.'

Another stab in the guts made Rakesh shiver.

Marshall frowned at him. 'You okay there?'

'Bit of an upset stomach.'

Marshall laughed. 'Those omelette sandwiches?'

'I'll be fine. Popped some Imodium on the way over.'

'Well, take it easy if you need to.'

'Will do, sir.'

Marshall tapped out a message on his phone. 'Cannon and Ball will be working their magic for a while in there. Assuming they ever find anything.'

'Cannon and Ball?'

'Never mind.'

'I take it Lennon isn't there?'

'Nope. Unless there's a secret hidey-hole up in the loft.' Marshall snorted. 'Craven's trying to find a ladder to go up there.'

Rakesh looked back at the house. Then down at the floor. Then again at the house. 'Listen, my guts are on fire. Do you mind if I go to the toilet?'

'Just as well it's not a crime scene.' Marshall winked. 'Though I suspect it'll be one soon.'

'Cheers, Rob.' Rakesh rushed up the path and weaved past the plainclothes officers working away in standard search patterns in the hall. The only doors from the hall led to a living room, an office and a kitchen. He stepped into the kitchen at the back of the house and looking across a lawn glowing bright under spotlights.

Two detectives emptying all of the cupboards like they were searching for a Mars bar just before a fasting day.

'Tell you, I've not seen this much Ken Hom stuff since my old dear passed away and I cleared her place.'

'Know what you mean. Boy must've had it made in the eighties, eh?'

Rakesh found the toilet.

Trouble was, a female officer was working in there.

Rakesh cleared his throat and had to fight the urge to dance from foot to foot. 'Sorry, I need to use the toilet.'

She took a look at him, then shrugged. 'Fine. There's nobody hiding in here. And no drugs.' She stepped out of the bathroom and gestured back in. 'Be my guest.'

'Thanks.' Rakesh ran in and locked the door behind him, his fingers struggling to secure the lock.

There.

He dropped his trousers and sat under the giant antique cistern, then dropped his guts, moaning with the release. 'Oh God.'

Then another splatter burned at his arse.

'*Fuuuuck!*'

And just as quickly, he was done.

He sat there, panting.

That was it. All over so quickly.

He reached for the toilet paper.

Then another burning spray blasted out.

'*Fuuuuuuuuuuck!*'

He leaned forward, cradling his head in his hands.

Covered in sweat.

What the hell?

His stomach burned and writhed and...

Stopped.

It was over.

He was panting, hard. Bloody hell. Everything burned down there, but it didn't feel like there was any more left to come out.

He gave it a few seconds, then reached again for the toilet paper and started wiping. It felt really tender and sore. He could imagine what Liam Inglis must be going through.

Scratch that – he had no idea what that felt like.

'Sounds like somebody's died in there.' The female officer's voice cut through the bathroom door.

'Jesus.' Craven's deep laugh rattled like a broken boiler. 'Don't spark the gas on the cooker or the whole house will go up. Now, have you seen a ladder?'

Rakesh finished and stood up, shutting the toilet lid so he didn't have to look at that abomination. He pulled his trousers back up and tugged on the chain, then walked over to the sink.

Nothing happened.

He went back and tugged the chain again.

Again, nothing.

He stepped onto the toilet lid and reached up to the overhead cistern. He eased off the lid and set it down on the sink, then reached a hand in.

No water in there – his finger just touched dry porcelain.

Then something plastic.

# CHAPTER TWENTY-FIVE

Craven's gangly frame was inside the bathroom, gloved up but not touching the haul of drugs and cash Rakesh had found.

The CSI holding them up looked monstrously bored, though. Another two of his colleagues stood on a set of ladders, one photographing and the other cataloguing the production of another two bricks of cocaine and one more of cash.

Too many people in one toilet, so Rakesh and Marshall stood back to give them room.

Craven left the room and smacked Rakesh on the arm. 'It's not true what they say about you, is it?'

Rakesh frowned at that. 'What do they say?'

'Never mind. This is good work, Rakesh.' Craven sniffed, then covered his nose. 'But that toilet pan is an absolute disgrace.' He barked out a laugh. 'Need to flush that somehow. We'll have to fill up those drums of water we found in the shed.' He took a glance back into the room and the corners of his nostrils turned up. 'What the hell had you been eating? Fried bread omelettes?'

'Omelette sandwiches.'

Craven laughed. 'That's not a thing. Is it?' He walked forward, nudging them into the kitchen.

Mukherjee was on the phone to someone. He glanced over, then looked away again. 'Will do, aye.' He ended his call and snapped his old-school folding phone shut, the kind of thing a drugs kingpin would use as a burner. Cheap and disposable. He pocketed it, but kept his hand in there. 'How's it looking?'

'An absolute disgrace.' Craven shot Rakesh a look, though the smile didn't go much of the way towards dispelling the derision at Rakesh's bowel movement. 'But we've got another two bricks of coke, guv, and one of cash.'

'Good stuff.' Mukherjee shook his head at Rakesh, but it was more surprise than derision. 'Amazing work. *Amazing.*' He smiled at Marshall. 'This lad's wasted in uniform.'

Marshall raised his eyebrows. 'It has been said.' He cleared his throat. 'Anyway, what's the plan here?'

'The plan?' Mukherjee blew air up his face. 'We like to operate without one. Keeps us flexible. And people can't get wind of what we're doing if we don't. But in terms of actions, I've just been on the phone to our lads staking out Dylan's house. He's not in – left about half an hour ago.'

Marshall folded his arms. 'Just after the incident at the theatre.'

'Indeed. Almost like he's meeting his brother.'

Rakesh rested against the counter by the sink. 'So it looks like both brothers are running away?'

Mukherjee looked over at him. 'That's one outcome. Could be lying low somewhere.'

'But we don't have any more likely locations, do we?'

'Correct.' Mukherjee rubbed at his eyes. 'Bloody tired.' A little yawn escaped his lips. 'Okay, we've got a few threads we can tug on, but we need to get your lot out hunting for this dude, okay?'

Rakesh looked over at Marshall. 'I'll need to take that up with Asher.'

'He'll be fine with it.' Marshall shrugged. 'It's what you've been doing for me, after all.'

Rakesh nodded, but he didn't like the implication of being passed from one boss to another. 'You know we're off duty soon, right?'

# CHAPTER TWENTY-SIX

Rakesh walked up the drive towards what remained of his team, all just standing around and chatting.

Bell was first to notice Rakesh. 'Shift's up soon, Sarge.'

'I know. Just raised that with DCI Marshall.' Rakesh joined them. 'There's overtime on offer until seven.'

Bell checked his watch. His forehead creased and a grin filled his face. 'Count me in.'

Helen nodded. 'And me.'

'Could do without it.' Ella sighed. 'But fine. In for a penny, in for a pound.'

'Thanks.' Rakesh shifted his gaze between them, one by one. 'Okay, now you're all on for another few hours of fun time, we need to track down both Lennon and Dylan.'

Bell folded his arms. 'Sure thing, Sarge. We getting any help?'

'Partly. Night shift have come on early, so we're clear from frontline response. And we've been asked to provide support to the MIT. So let's reconvene outside Lennon's home and see what we can unearth there.'

'Already been there, Sarge.' Bell shared a look with Helen, then shrugged. 'But fine, you're the boss.' He got into his car.

'See you there, Sarge.' Ella got in the passenger side of the other patrol car.

Rakesh sighed, rubbing at his guts.

Helen was still there, head tilted to the side. 'You okay?'

Rakesh smiled at her. 'I'm fine now. Just...'

'You need some more of my Imodium?'

'No, that horse has bolted. Mercifully.'

'Too much information, Sarge.' Helen got into the passenger side of ECC18.

Rakesh watched Bell drive off, then got behind the wheel of ECC15. Hard to escape the fact that his guts were burning again. He didn't think he needed to go back inside, but still...

Helen and Ella were still sitting there. Why hadn't they driven off? Arguing over who was driving?

He reached for the radio. 'Control, this is ECC15, over.'

'Receiving, over.'

'Can you put out a call for both Lennon Blackwell and Dylan Blackwell? Latter is driving a purple Tesla model 3. Over.'

'Noted, over.'

'Do you need the plates? Over.'

'Got them on file from your earlier request, Sergeant. Over.'

'Thank you. Over and out.'

Rakesh sat back, squirming in his seat. The car was melting or at least felt like it was. He needed to take something for this pain, that was for sure.

The radio crackled and squawked. 'All units, be on the lookout for a Tesla model 3, with licence plate SK73—'

Someone chapped on the window.

Mukherjee and Craven stood there, both grinning from ear to ear.

Rakesh wound down the window and smiled at them. 'What's up?'

Mukherjee held his gaze. 'You've got to try a bit harder than that, mate.'

'What are you talking about?'

'This is detective work, sunshine.' Craven tapped his nose. 'We're the heroes. You lot are the zeroes. Now bugger off and do your job.'

The pair of arseholes walked over to their car, laughing and joking as they went.

Rakesh wound the window back up and put his car in gear.

It stalled.

*Bastard thing.*

*Take a second...*

He put the car in neutral, then sucked in a deep breath. Those wankers were inside his head. And he hated people being inside his head, especially bell ends like them.

Who the hell did they think they were?

He'd just done his job, put out the basic request and they'd...

Wankers.

Absolute wankers.

Wankers everywhere!

He twisted the key in the ignition to the off position, then started it up again.

Helen was walking over.

Rakesh wound the window down again. 'What's up?'

Helen rested against the door and handed him the blister pack of Imodium. 'You should just ignore those pricks.'

'I am.' Rakesh took the pills. 'Thanks for this.'

Helen scowled over at the car. 'I mean, who do they think they are? *Heroes*? *Them*? Drugs cops are always bent. Always.'

Rakesh maintained his smile. 'It's fine, Helen. I've dealt with way worse.'

Helen looked back at him, her eyes narrowed. 'Sure, but the way those pricks talked to you boils my piss like I've got thrush again.'

Rakesh laughed. 'That's a lovely image.'

'Aye, I'm full of—'

The radio blasted out a load of chatter.

'Hang on a sec.' Rakesh reached over, hoping it was a sighting of Lennon or Dylan.

'All units.' A female cop's voice, her breath shallow and her voice high. 'Requesting urgent back-up to Forth View Crescent in Danderhall. Over.'

Helen frowned. 'Hang on. Isn't Forth View Crescent where that missing lassie lives?'

# CHAPTER TWENTY-SEVEN

Rakesh was first out onto the street and it wasn't exactly difficult to tell which address they were interested in.

An angry mob had assembled outside a semi-detached home, the fresh harling glowing under streetlights, even way past the witching hour. The waist-height chain-link fence had been no match for the gang, who congregated in the middle of the lawn. All men of a certain age, dressed in jeans and sports gear, all chanting:

'Liar! Liar! Liar, liar, liar!'

Sure enough, Polly Ward and some of her squad were defending the house, blocking the front door. Six of them spread across the lawn, batons drawn.

Not so much a Mexican stand-off as a Scottish one.

Neither side moved forward, but neither moved back.

Polly made eye contact with Rakesh and bobbed her chin. A wave would've inflamed the situation.

Rakesh turned to his team. 'Guard the entrance, okay? Let's box them in.'

'Sarge.' The three of them spread into a loose formation across the lawn, but kept a distance from the mob.

'Police!' Rakesh weaved his through the crowd. 'Police coming through!' He made it to the front and stood next to Polly on the doorstep.

'Fucking hell.' Polly waved at the gang. A strand of hair dangled free from her tight ponytail. 'This lot swarmed out of nowhere.'

'Have they attacked?'

'Not yet. Just a ton of trespassing. And a protest.'

'Against what?'

'Search me.'

'Liar! Liar! Liar, liar, liar!'

Rakesh swept his gaze through the crowd of drunken hooligans, but didn't recognise anyone.

'Liar! Liar! Liar, liar, liar!'

Polly nudged Rakesh on the arm and it made him jump. 'Dawn's mum took us to her dad's grave. Thought Dawn might've gone there. Nope.'

Rakesh pointed at the crowd. 'What do they think she's lying about?'

'Your guess is as good as mine, mate.'

'Do they think she's killed Dawn?'

'I've thought that. Who knows. Social media will be full of armchair detectives who've already sussed it out.' Polly shook her head. '*Total* bullshit.'

Rakesh scanned the crowd. The faces of drunk thugs, all filled with bile and hatred, which was usually directed towards the wrong target. And it always had a target, no matter how spurious the logic.

Wait a second.

Johnnie stood in the middle of the throng, cupping his hands around his mouth. 'Liar, liar, liar!'

Rakesh nudged Polly on the arm. 'I know the ringleader.'

'Who?'

'Him.' Rakesh pointed at Johnnie. 'John Kincaid. At least, that was according to the barman.'

'You believe him?'

'Come on, Polly, you know the rules... Next time, the police don't arrive on time when he calls.'

'Understood. What happened?'

'He was in a skirmish in Niddrie.'

Polly shot him a glare. 'And you let him *go*?'

'He was on the receiving end of said skirmish.' Rakesh broke off from their defensive line and approached him, raising his hands ever so slowly. 'Sir, I need to—'

Johnnie arched his back and shouted, 'Ann! You're a dirty hooer!'

Rakesh grabbed his arm tightly. 'Sir, I need you to—'

Johnnie shook his sleeve free. 'Who the hell do you think you are?'

'The police.' Rakesh got in his face. 'Need I remind you that her child's missing? I'm asking you to—'

Johnnie laughed. 'Aye, and who do you think's taken her, eh? She's shagging a fucking asylum seeker. Filthy bastard from Syria! That's who's taken her!'

Rakesh was struggling to hold himself together in the face of his hatred and rage. 'Sir, we need you to back away from—'

A man to the left of Johnnie pulled his arm back, then launched something towards the house.

Rakesh twisted around and followed the flaming arc as the object swung towards the roof, dowsing the tiles and the front wall in a spreading flame.

A Molotov cocktail.

Bloody hell...

'Right, you!' Rakesh launched himself at the fire-starter and took him down, pinning him to the ground.

Johnnie and his mates started jostling him, pulling his arms back and dragging him away.

Polly waved at her team. 'Arrest them!'

The squad gave up playing nice and descended on the gang, clubbing away with batons.

Rakesh grabbed his cuffs from his belt and slapped them onto the fire-starter's wrists. He looked up and saw his trio approaching from the rear, corralling the thugs into a tight area in the corner. He stood up and nodded at Bell. 'George, arrest him! And call in the fire service!'

'Sarge.' Bell grabbed hold of the fire-starter with an almost unwarranted degree of force – then again, the scumbag had just firebombed the home of a mother at her wits' end.

Flames licked at the gutters, melting the plastic pipes.

Rakesh followed Polly inside the house. It already reeked of smoke – something had caught fire upstairs, probably.

Polly raced ahead, deeper into the home.

Rakesh took the first door on the right. A living room.

A woman cowered under the window, probably the worst place she could hide.

'Polly! In here!' Rakesh turned back and raised his hands. 'Hi, I'm a police officer. We need to get you out of here.'

Polly charged in, then ran over to the window. 'Come on, Ann. Let's go.'

Ann scowled up at her. 'What's going on?'

'The place is on fire. Need to get you outside, okay?' Polly offered her a hand. 'Come on.'

Ann looked at it. 'But...'

'It's okay. We've got them.'

Ann reluctantly took her hand and let her winch her up to standing.

Rakesh went first, leading Ann and Polly back outside into the smoke-filled night.

The squad had subdued some of the gang, with the remainder running off through the streets.

Ella had the Molotov chucker in cuffs, with Bell and Helen struggling to contain the raging bull that was Johnnie.

'Get off me, you fascist cunts!'

Polly walked Ann over to Rakesh's squad car and put her in the back seat. 'Let's get you somewhere safe.'

# CHAPTER TWENTY-EIGHT

Wearing those trousers, coupled with the utility belt, for more than a full shift made Rakesh feel like he'd been cut in two. He unclipped the belt and stuffed it into his locker – hopefully the last time he'd need it tonight – then strolled back through to the station's processing area, all lit up as though it was midday but he was yawning like he was getting up for a pee in the middle of the night.

Blasting his eyeballs with fake light must've been the only way Wilson could cope with back or night shifts. And the flurry of activity coming from behind the desk, clicking keys and hammering fingers, showed it was proving to be effective.

Rakesh led Johnnie and his big pal in, helped by Ella and Helen. The second-hand booze wafting off them was enough to start a fire in here. Away from the conflagration, the alcohol turned from pissed-up aggression into early-onset hangover – they weren't putting up any fight now.

Wilson looked up. He narrowed his eyes, then looked back down again, shaking his head. 'I *knew* I shouldn't have walked under that ladder this morning...' He sighed, then looked back up at them.

Rakesh stopped by the desk. 'Can you process these two?'

'What's the charge?'

'Wilful fire-raising.' Rakesh motioned to the still-unnamed fire-starter. 'This one lobbed a Molotov cocktail at the house of a woman whose daughter's missing. Pair of charmers, aren't you?'

Johnnie and his mate hung their heads even lower, losing themselves in their almighty hangovers.

'Will do.' Wilson grabbed a form. 'Name.'

The fire-starter stayed focused on his shoes.

'Mate, I need a name.'

'Don't know it.'

Wilson laughed. 'Aye, aye. My granny always told me the old ones are the best. Name.'

'Martha Farquhar.'

'Now. We can do this the hard way or the easy way. Last chance or it goes down as John Doe and that cell with the leak over the bed is yours.'

'Fuck you.'

'John Doe it is, then...' Wilson stopped and laughed.

'You've just set fire to someone's home. Why the hell should I care what happens to you?' He pointed over to the corner. 'Helen, Ella, can you hold them here for a second? Cheers.' He watched them walk them over, then beckoned Rakesh closer. 'Do me a favour, would you?'

Rakesh stayed where he was. 'Depends what it is.'

'Was just about to get that Keegan kid through, but processing those two is going to delay things.'

'What were you bringing him through for?'

'Got his court date, so I was going to release him now. Any chance you could…?'

Rakesh didn't have to think too long on that. A chance to impart some post-cell wisdom to the kid… 'Fair enough. Which cell?'

'Six.'

'On it.' Rakesh took one last scornful look at Johnnie and the fire-starter, both looking very sorry for themselves, then pushed through into the cells.

Someone was singing a Corries song Rakesh only knew through a cousin's wife. Her ironic love of the old folk singers wasn't shared by the passionate vocalist here – it was purely heartfelt, though the love was mangled by an inability to hold a note for longer than a beat. And it wasn't even 'Flower of Scotland', but that one that had something to do with Dundee and the West Port. Whatever the West Port was. Dundee had docks, but why they needed to be hooked was beyond Rakesh…

He walked along to the end and the singing stopped. Must be his footsteps and the promise of liberty.

Keegan's neighbour was looking out at him. Gabriel McInvar. Lost eyes, incapable of understanding the magnitude of his actions.

Rakesh opened the door to Keegan's and the singing started up again.

Keegan was sitting on his bunk, knees pulled up to his chest. He looked over at Rakesh, then back. Then doubled back to stare at him again. 'You?'

'Me.' Rakesh beckoned him out. 'Come on.'

'What?'

'You're getting out.'

Keegan scowled at him. 'But... You arrested me?'

'We did. You don't automatically go from an arrest to a custodial sentence. It depends on the magnitude of the crime. Yours was assaulting a police officer, which is pretty serious, but not serious enough to keep you off the street. You're allowed out, but you will have to attend your court hearing in two weeks, otherwise that'll be a much more serious crime.'

Keegan frowned. 'Are you going to kick the shit out of me? Is that it?'

'It'll feel like it.' Rakesh smiled. 'I'm going to make you fill out a load of forms.'

'And if I don't?'

'If you don't sign the forms, you don't get out. End of story. There's no other option. If you leave now, you can go back to kipping on your pal Shaft's sofa. Either way, you're giving me an address and you're appearing in court.'

A rousing chorus of another Corries song started up again. 'Flower of Scotland' this time.

Rakesh couldn't have choreographed it any better.

Keegan looked at the door, then at the floor. His forehead pulsed for a few seconds, then he got up. 'Fine, I'll fill out your stupid forms.' He walked over to the door.

Rakesh stepped back and led him back past the cells, then opened the door leading to the processing area.

He had to drag Keegan back away from it.

Wilson led Johnnie and his fire-starter mate through into the cells, supported by Ella and Helen. Neither of them made eye contact with Keegan.

Wilson waved a hand behind them. 'Papers are on the desk.'

'Cheers.' Rakesh waited until they were far enough away, then led Keegan out and over to the desk.

Keegan kept glancing back towards the door. 'Glad to get away from those wankers.'

'Stay there.' Rakesh slipped behind the desk and into Wilson's domain. He scanned around for the paperwork, but the desk was an abomination. Took Rakesh a few seconds to sift through the discarded pages and several days' worth of *Metro*s, open at the puzzles page.

So much for the papers being on the—

There.

Rakesh checked over the page. 'Keegan Tait, right?'

'Aye.' Keegan stared him down. 'What of it?'

'Did I say there was anything?' Rakesh looked around for a pen, which meant navigating through the rubbish Wilson kept on the desk all over again.

A nibbled black biro sat on a folder with Dawn O'Keefe's photo stapled to it.

Could he really use that?

Not that there were any alternatives – he'd left his belt in his locker.

No choice – he had to use the nibbled one. He picked up the pen and looked at the photo of Dawn.

Something about it sang to him...

He opened the folder and sifted through the pages. A couple more photos of Dawn – her at a family barbecue, her posing as a lost girl in a park.

*Oh, shit.*

# CHAPTER TWENTY-NINE

Back in the cells, Rakesh let out a deep breath, then passed the paperwork through the bars.

Happy Meal took it, but scowled at him. 'What's this?'

'Your paperwork.'

Happy Meal looked at it. 'You've scored out my name?'

'Indeed. I had to correct it to your actual name. Dawn Ashley O'Keefe.'

'What the fuck are you talking about?'

'Also known as Gabriel McInvar.' Rakesh put the pen down on the page. 'You've been lying to us, Gabriel.'

'Lying? I've been telling the world my truth!'

'As you're now living as Gabriel McInvar, that's the name I'll address you as. But legally, I have to fill out the forms under your birth name. Dawn Ashley O'Keefe, right?'

Gabriel's eyes went wide. 'You're deadnaming me, bitch?'

'I suggest you refrain from using terms like that against a serving officer.' Rakesh fixed him with a hard stare. 'I didn't deadname you, Gabriel. I was incredibly careful not to. Believe me, I'm an ally.'

Gabriel's foot was tapping, hard and fast. 'If you're an ally, can't you just let me go?'

'I also have to be an ally to the officer your fireworks injured.'

'Fuck.'

'You're fourteen and still a minor, despite what you've been getting up to.' Rakesh went back to filling out the form. 'How long have you been living as Gabriel?'

'Few months.'

'Does your mother know?'

Gabriel looked away, then gave a slight shake of the head. 'She wouldn't understand. Dumb bitch doesn't care about me.'

'That's not true. You ran away yesterday, Gabriel. Or you just didn't attend school. Your mother called it in this morning and we've had half of Edinburgh out looking for you.' Rakesh waited for Gabriel to look back, then locked eyes with him. 'Or at least for who she knows you as. And the irony is you're in a cell here, under a different name, pretending to be eighteen.'

'Can do what I want. It's a free country.'

'Freedom comes with responsibilities. And also with

guardrails. You're fourteen, Gabriel. You're not old enough to live away from home.'

'Fuck do you care? Going to jail anyway.'

Rakesh ran a hand through his hair. 'You might be over the age of criminal responsibility, Gabriel, but you won't be housed in an adult male prison. It'll be a young offenders' institution.' He sighed. 'And your gender is, of course, going to make things difficult.'

Gabriel snarled. 'Fuck's that supposed to mean?'

'Because you haven't legally transitioned.'

'Can do what I want.'

'No. It's a matter for you and your mother, as your legal guardian to—'

'*Fuck* her, man. Stupid fucking bitch.'

All the aggro and attitude was borrowed second-hand from hip-hop records and gangster films. And from people like Keegan Tait. The posture, the poses, all of it was stolen.

'Gabriel, you told us your mother was dead.'

'Might as well be.'

'You remember your friend Johnnie?'

'Who?'

'Big guy.' Rakesh held out his hand at a certain height. 'You spat on him.'

'What about him?'

'He had someone lob a firebomb at your home.'

'What?' Gabriel's mouth fell open. 'Because of me?'

'Do they know who you really are?'

'No. Nobody does. Told them I'm from Inverness.' Gabriel sniffed. 'Why were they there?'

'They were chanting "Liar" at your mum.'

'I don't know why.'

'Okay, Gabriel. I'm choosing to believe you here. But you're moving in some incredibly dangerous circles. Why did you do it?'

'Do what? Transition?'

'No. But you need to work *with* your mum, okay? There's a standard process in this country to help in situations like this.' Rakesh left a pause, hoping the words sank in. 'But you assaulting a police officer isn't going to help matters any. And hanging out with a gang. Especially one like that.'

'You wouldn't understand.'

'Try me, Gabriel. I'm here to listen to people as much as enforce the law.' Rakesh still remembered what it felt like to be that age, to have all those conflicting feelings, all those chemicals and pheromones confusing your developing brain. 'Did that gang make you feel like you belonged?'

Gabriel stared hard at him, then tears welled up in his eyes. He collapsed against the wall, then slid down it, crying. 'Fuck.'

'I'm sorry for what you're going through, Gabriel. I have the deepest sympathies. But whatever it is, you need to get off this path of violence you're on. You're still young. Too young.' Rakesh opened the door and beckoned him out.

Gabriel frowned, then jumped at the chance and walked over to the door.

Rakesh stopped him with a hand. 'You've got a chance to change things, once you've paid the price for this. Otherwise you *will* end up in an adult prison. And people in jail aren't tolerant of trans people. It'd be a bad situation for you, one the institution isn't yet capable of righting.'

# CHAPTER THIRTY

Rakesh was behind the wheel, taking it quickly along the road, then having to slow for the slaloming path through a housing estate in the Jewel.

Gabriel was in the back, staring out of the window. Mouth open. He wiped fresh tears from his cheeks and looked over at Rakesh for a few seconds, then back at the window.

He looked so young. Not exactly feminine, but soft. Not fit for a world of hard men, no matter how much he thought he wanted it.

Fourteen was no age to get into criminality.

And Rakesh was no child psychologist, but he could only imagine the tumultuous events that had led Gabriel down this dark path, step by step. Or maybe he'd just sprinted down it, heading towards a gang that offered family he maybe didn't feel at home.

Either way, being in a gang offered certainty – you followed the rules, you got on. You got the one thing he didn't feel he had – respect. And it offered a clear hierarchy – you show off to this person, they'll reward you.

And at that age, time was still an abstract concept. Days were mostly spent in the eternal *now* of childhood, whether in front of *Fortnite*, *FIFA* or *Call of Duty*, or out and about with friends from school or elsewhere. The days passed and it was all about now.

But Gabriel was on a precipice, when the now started to fill with the dread of an uncertain future or the painful regret over a squandered past.

Shooting fireworks at the police was just banter. Who knew it would lead to a custodial sentence?

Wilson's phrase kept rattling around his brain.

*Can't do the time, don't do the crime.*

Not that Rakesh suspected the sentencing would be draconian. Any lawyer worth their salt would get the child psychologists to assess and then testify on his behalf.

But Liam's injuries were irrefutable. It would set a bad precedent if police officers were suddenly fair game for anyone with trauma in their past.

One final turning and Rakesh pulled up on a quiet street, parking behind ECC12.

Rakesh got out and opened the back door, then offered a hand to Gabriel. 'Here we are. You're free to go. Just remember the terms of your undertaking.'

Gabriel rubbed at his cheeks, then got out. He sucked in a deep breath. 'I did listen to what you said, you know?'

'Which bit?'

'About this path I'm on. The violence. The hate. The destruction. It's... It's not me. I'm a boy. A man. But... I hate what I'm doing.' Gabriel stared at Rakesh. 'Can I see that cop?'

'I can arrange for you to visit, Gabriel, but that's on the condition that you'll apologise to him.'

'Of course I will. Please. I hate what I did. I didn't think... I...'

The house door opened and Ann O'Keefe stepped out into the night. Polly was alongside her.

Ann stood there, her hand covering her mouth. She rushed over to them and wrapped Gabriel in a big cuddle. 'Dawn... Where the hell have you been?'

Gabriel pushed her away, but Ann was determined. Then he gave in and let her hug him tight.

Polly appeared, nodding at Rakesh.

Ann finally let Gabriel break off the hug.

Rakesh nodded at her. 'Do you mind I have a word?'

Ann looked him up and down. Then rubbed at her forehead. She patted Gabriel on the arm. 'Dawn, can you go to your auntie's house?'

'It's Gabriel, Mum.'

'Right. Of course. Need to speak to the officer here alone.'

Gabriel took a last look at Rakesh, holding it as his lips trembled, then he let Polly walk him back over to the house. He stopped at the door and took one last look at Rakesh, then slipped inside.

Ann was staring at the ground. 'I didn't know.'

'Of course.' Rakesh waited for her to look up at him. She didn't. 'Are you okay there?'

'What kind of question is that?' Ann shook her head. 'My fucking house is on fire!'

'I gather that's under control now and there should be no lingering damage.'

'Right.'

'I understand how much of a shock this must be about... About your child.'

'Do you?'

Rakesh held her gaze. 'Of course I do. You're contending with multiple things here. Revelations about your child. And worse, about their actions.'

'I didn't know about Dawn. How she's... Gabriel... He's... Christ.' She clawed at her hair, like she wanted to tear it all out. 'This is melting my brain.'

'It's fairly common. You're not alone.'

'It's...' She waved a hand at Polly. 'Your colleague... Polly... She said those men thought I'd been sleeping with an asylum seeker?'

'That's correct.'

'Why would they think that?'

'I was going to ask you the same question.'

'It's bullshit.'

'They thought this asylum seeker had taken Dawn.'

'Jesus Christ. This... These... Those fucks. Who was it?'

'The leader's name was John Kincaid.'

'Him.'

'You know him?'

'My dad went to school with him.'

'Your father?'

'Right. I mean, he was seventeen when... When he knocked up my mum. That's the only way of putting it. In fairness, he's actually been there for me, for better or for worse. Always stood up to Johnnie and those pricks he hangs out with. Old bastards...' She glared at him. 'I'm not seeing anyone. Dawn was hard enough work as it is.'

'Why would they think that?'

'Because they're racist arseholes.' Ann rubbed at her nose. 'Listen, I work for a charity in Edinburgh. We help people get the help they need. Asylum seekers, refugees who've slipped through the net. People who had the misfortune to be born here. We don't do the helping, but we triage it. You know, like in medicine, like when you're in A&E?'

Rakesh nodded. 'I understand that.'

'All we do is put them in touch with other charities who help with that kind of thing.'

'That's good work you're doing.'

'Is it? Because it gets harder every day. Especially when scumbags like Johnnie think you're doing other things. Just trying to do some good in the world after... After the start I've had. Having Dawn when I was fifteen. And they think I'm... They think someone's abducted Dawn... Christ, I'm doing such a bad job of this.'

Rakesh let her have a moment's peace – probably the first since the phone call about her child not turning up at school.

She swept her hair away from her eyes. 'I don't know what I'm going to do.'

'About what?'

'Dawn... This Gabriel stuff isn't the hard bit. It's... What she did to that poor cop. Polly told me.' She pointed over at the house, where Polly stood with Gabriel in the living-room window. 'The thing is, I didn't know what the hell Dawn was up to half the time. Since she was twelve, she's been hanging out with some wild kids. Out at all hours. And I tried everything I could, but it's impossible to keep her in. I was awake most of the night wondering where she was. Biggest fear I had was worrying if she was going to get herself pregnant like I did. I'm twenty-nine. I shouldn't have to deal with this, should I?'

'There's no "should" about it. We all face different battles.'

'Right. And I didn't know she was running with gangs.

I didn't know she thought she was a boy.' Ann wiped away a fresh tear. 'I wish she'd *told* me. I wish *he'd* told me. Christ. I can see it all now. She padded herself out with thick jackets and hoodies and layers upon layers, made her look bigger than she is. Those pricks she was hanging out with... She's in a gang, right?' She slapped her forehead. 'He is.'

'That appears to be the case, yes. Gabriel will face charges over that.'

Ann looked over at the house. The window was empty now. 'Can they fix her? Him.'

'The criminality is something he'll work on with a child psychologist. It's not a magic pill. He will have to open up to them and engage with their process.'

'And the... other stuff?'

'Whatever form that takes, you owe it to Dawn or Gabriel or whoever they present as to be the best mum you can be.'

'Not doing a great job of that, am I?' Her laugh was softened by tears. 'Listen, I don't care about all that other shite. Dawn or Gabriel. I just want my kid to be happy.' She shut her eyes.

'Given Gabriel's age, it's unlikely he'll face a lengthy sentence. But you need to use this as an opportunity to reconnect.'

'Easier said than done.' Ann trudged over to the house, her head hanging heavy on her shoulders.

Rakesh's radio chirruped.

'Taylor to Siyal, over.'

What was it now?

He reached over for his radio. 'Siyal here. Over.'

'Need a word with you, Sarge. We're at the Asda at the Jewel. Over.'

## CHAPTER THIRTY-ONE

The supermarket glowed in the darkness, the giant triangular entrance still with a reasonable footfall of traffic at this time of night. Twenty-four-hour shops were the domain of shift workers, like Rakesh was now, and offered employment to those who hated working in daylight. Vampires, maybe, or just night owls. Rakesh himself had taken to shopping here – pushing a trolley around at half three after a back shift like this.

He followed the road towards a broken-down bus at the far side of the Asda car park and pulled in next to another squad car, driver's door to driver's door.

The other car wound down the window.

Helen was behind the wheel, with Ella shivering in the cold behind her.

Rakesh leaned over. 'Seriously, if you want to pop into Asda for a sandwich, then just do it.'

'It's not about that.' Helen entered the shop but her pace slowed. 'We've been looking into this... Dawn's mother's boyfriend. The one those racist arseholes said was from Syria.'

'Okay. And?'

'Well, he works here.'

'She just told me she wasn't seeing anyone.'

'Right. And that's just tallied with what he told us.'

'Go on?'

'Muhammad Bakri, a refugee from Syria. Given the right to remain here. Works in the Asda on the night fill. Reason he's a refugee is he's gay. His boyfriend was killed there and he fled. Ann works for a charity and helps people who've slipped through the net. Like him. Helped him get this job.' She looked over at the store. 'Poor woman, eh? Doing a good job like that and having your kid go missing? Then... All this shite online.'

'What shite?'

'Right. Well. We spoke to some guys I know in the social media team in Gartcosh. Looks like someone had been spreading rumours. You know how it is? Even named him as Muhammad Bakri. Said he was from Syria and he'd been sleeping with Ann. He'd even been grooming Dawn. And he'd killed her and the mum knew all about it. Anyway, the social media team in Gartcosh will follow up in the morning. Hopefully be able to charge that arsehole with inciting racial hatred.'

'That's good work, Helen.'

'Thanks, Sarge.' Helen winced. 'Sarge, I'm Hank Marvin. Mind if I pop into Asda and get a sandwich?'

'Could do with something myself.' Rakesh pointed at the shop. 'We're miles away here.'

Helen shrugged. 'Always park at the other side of the car park.'

'In case someone spots us?'

Helen tapped her smartwatch. 'To get more steps in.'

Rakesh hadn't joined that cult, but he could understand the desire to constantly achieve something towards your goal. 'Ella, do you want something?'

'I'm good.' She shook her head. 'But thanks.'

Rakesh wound up his window, then got out and followed Helen across the car park and into the superstore – felt like he'd been walking for hours just to get this far.

Helen walked up to the takeaway food section, near the cigarette counter.

And they weren't the only cops in there.

PC Simon Lawson and Tommy Braithwaite looked like twin brothers, just the shade of ginger on Lawson's skinhead distinguishing them.

Lawson lugged a bag full of food towards them and stopped, resting it at his feet. 'Excellent work there, Sarge. Finding that Dawn lassie. I mean, she was hiding in plain sight, but...'

'Thank you, Si. And you were central to taking down John Kincaid.'

'All in a day's work, Sarge.' Lawson gave a stoic nod. 'Listen, we've been told to clear off home after we drop off everyone's second pieces.' He held up the bag. 'Unless you need us back on shift?'

'Nah.' Rakesh stepped out of their way. 'I'll see you back at the ranch on Thursday. Day shift.'

'Day shift. Have a good weekend, Sarge.' Lawson walked off with Braithwaite.

Helen was crouched in front of the sandwich chiller. She looked up. 'You want something?'

Rakesh picked out a sports drink. Something that'd get his electrolytes back in order after his… incident at the house.

Helen snatched it off him, then scanned it all through the self-scan till. Her sandwich was a reduced-price egg mayonnaise.

Rakesh felt something rumble deep inside his guts. 'Is that a joke?'

'What?' Helen picked up her sandwich. 'Oh, no. Sorry, it's the only one that was reduced. I hate paying full price.' She tapped her card against the reader, then walked off through the shop. 'Was that Lawson?'

'Right. With Braithwaite. Sent them home.'

'Is our overtime still good?'

'Aye. Still a fair amount left to do. We haven't

managed to locate either Blackwell brother. And that's still our number one task.'

'Doing everything but finding them, eh?' Helen passed him his drink as they stepped outside.

Rakesh stopped to take a sip. He was gasping and only just realised now. He swallowed down a glug of sickening sugary orange juice.

Helen folded her arms, clutching her sandwich tight to her chest. 'Should be getting off shift now, shouldn't we?'

Rakesh finished his drink and looked around for a recycling bin.

There.

'Back in a sec.' He doubled back towards the bin by the entrance, then stopped dead.

A Tesla model 3 sat a few spaces away. Purple or navy – hard to tell under the lights. Nobody in it.

Rakesh frowned at it, then hurried off. 'Come on.'

'What is it?'

Rakesh raced over to the other side of the broken-down bus, then pulled out his notebook from his belt and flicked to the latest page. He noted down the plate, then went to the previous page and compared it.

Helen joined him. 'Sarge, what is it?'

Rakesh looked back at the shop. 'That's Dylan's car.'

# CHAPTER THIRTY-TWO

Rakesh felt like a sitting duck here.

Stuck in his squad car, wedged behind the broken-down bus. If he stretched to the side, he could sort of see the entrance to the Asda.

No sign of Dylan, but his car was still sitting there.

Rakesh put his radio to his mouth. 'ECC15 to ECC16, over.'

'ECC16 receiving.' Lawson's voice was like a crisp, clear morning. 'Safe to talk. Over.'

'Do you still have eyes on the rear entrance? Over.'

'Still here, Sarge. Parked up with a good view of the front entrance through a pair of binocs. We have very good sight lines. Over.'

'Okay, let me know the second that changes. Over.'

'Will do. Over and out.'

Rakesh put the radio down and looked around.

Two cars swept into the car park, then headed towards him and pulled up next to him, boxing him in.

Marshall got out of the first car.

Mukherjee and Craven stayed in the second.

Rakesh got out and walked over. 'Still no sign of them.'

'Great.' Marshall was scanning the area. 'But the car's still here?'

Rakesh nodded.

'He's been there, what, twenty-five minutes?' Marshall looked over at the shop. 'He must've clocked us.'

'Or he's doing a week's shop in there?'

'Are you being sarcastic?'

'No.' Rakesh shrugged. 'Got aisles of clothes. Toiletries. Even some camping gear. Everything you need to disappear.'

Marshall sighed. 'Could be that, I suppose.'

A squad car pulled up and Bell got out. 'Sorry, Sarge. Wilson needed a hand with a drunk singing the Corries.'

'The *Corries*?' Marshall frowned. 'Bloody hell.'

'Aye. 'Flower of Scotland' then 'Bonnie Dundee'. Think it's based on a poem by Sir Walter Scott, sir. You're based down in the Borders, aren't you?'

'Aye. Recently lost an officer to an incident near his old house. Abbotsford. Dropped on his head from a moving van.'

'Jesus Christ.'

'Aye, that's about the size of it.'

Rakesh's radio crackled.

'Sarge.' Helen's voice, soft and low. 'Eyes on the prize. Front entrance.'

Rakesh walked over to the bus, then peered around the side.

Dylan was standing at the front door. Looking around, taking a drink from a bottle of Dr Pepper. He carried a bag towards the Tesla.

'Spread out, but don't move in on him.' Marshall started walking. 'Give him a few seconds. Lennon might be here too.'

Rakesh set off, keeping low as he made his way over – not easy when you're in a deserted car park. A pair of vans let him stand up tall. He peered around the side.

Lennon walked out of the front door, lugging two heavy bags.

Mukherjee ran forward. 'Go! Go! Go!'

'Bloody nitwit.' Marshall sprinted off, his heavy frame making his feet slap across the tarmac.

Rakesh followed him over towards the Blackwell brothers.

Lennon swung around, realising just how screwed he was, and dropped his bags.

Dylan was over by the car, eyes wide.

Lennon reached into a bag and pulled out a five-pack of tuna tins. He hurled it at Craven and it clonked him on the head.

Craven tumbled over and everyone slowed down.

Marshall raised a hand. 'Stop!'

Everyone stopped and gave them space.

Rakesh overtook Marshall and approached Dylan, his baton raised. He lashed forward with it.

Dylan dodged out of the way of Rakesh's strike, then grabbed him under the armpits and legs.

Everything tipped upside down and Dylan body-slammed Rakesh onto his car.

He landed on his back, winding him again. Just like in the theatre. Pain erupted all the way up his back.

He tried to sit up and caught sight of Lennon throwing a tin of soup at Bell, just missing him.

Someone grabbed Rakesh from behind and hauled him off the car.

Dylan, pressing a knife against Rakesh's throat. 'Let me go or this cunt gets it!'

Marshall approached, hands up. 'It's okay, Dylan. Nothing bad's going to happen to you.'

Dylan dug the knife into Rakesh's skin. 'I know, because you're letting me go!'

Bell stepped forward. 'You haven't got the balls to do it, have you?'

Rakesh raised his hands. 'I know he doesn't. He's just protecting his brother. I get it.' He craned his neck back to look at Dylan. 'Let me go before you do something you regret.'

'Come on, Dylan.' Bell raised his hands. 'How far do you think you'll get? About a mile down the road, you'll have a ton of—'

'Shut up!' Dylan pressed the steel against Rakesh's throat. 'Shut the fuck up!'

'Shit or get off the pot, pal.' Bell crouched low, hands raised. 'Because I don't think you're going to do it, are you?'

'Do you want me to kill him? Is that it?'

In a blur, Bell blasted a tin of soup at Rakesh's head.

He ducked low.

Dylan didn't.

Something thunked behind him and Dylan went down.

The knife clattered to the ground.

Rakesh swung around.

Bell pinned him down, hauling his arm up his back, then started searching him. 'He's got about a grand in cash on him. And two passports.' He snapped out his cuffs. 'Dylan Blackwell, I'm arresting you for the possession of—'

Behind Bell, Mukherjee dodged a thrown tin. It landed on the ground. He grabbed it and threw it back at Lennon. It clonked off Lennon's head and he went down.

Mukherjee raised both arms in the air. 'Howzat!'

Helen leapt into action and pushed Lennon onto his front.

Rakesh stood there, rubbing his throat. He expected to see blood, but his fingers came back dry.

Marshall wrapped an arm around his shoulders and led him away. 'You okay there?'

'I'm fine.'

'It's just, you had a—'

'Said I'm fine, Rob.'

'Okay.'

'I want to interview him.'

'Not going to happen.' Marshall shook his head. 'Remember, you're not a detective anymore.'

'I know, but—'

'But nothing. You've got a ton of paperwork to file here. Let me lead the interview and I'll come and see you afterwards, okay?'

Rakesh knew he didn't have a choice in the matter.

# CHAPTER THIRTY-THREE

During his career, Acting DCI Rob Marshall had been in rooms with monsters several times. Notorious serial killers who'd murdered people the length and breadth of the UK, employing various murder methods and for various reasons, usually unknown to even themselves.

Lennon Blackwell wasn't in that category.

Those men – and they were all men, with one notable exception – could handle themselves in a situation like this. They knew how to manipulate and play people. That had kept Marshall and his colleagues on their toes for years, requiring deep psychological strategies to get inside their heads.

Lennon definitely wasn't in that category either. He looked at Marshall. 'I don't know.'

Marshall had only been in this station once that he

could think of and the interview room was much bigger than the ones he was used to down in Galashiels, with enough space for all three participants to be able to stretch out. 'You don't know...'

'He doesn't know...' Craven rested his elbows on the table and leaned forward, acting like a bored teenager forced to watch an educational film about malaria in the Ivory Coast during geography. 'Okay, so how about we focus on your whereabouts from when you got the taxi from this station to when our fellow officers found you at your place of work?'

'Why?'

'Just humour me, pal, eh?'

Lennon frowned. 'I went to Dylan's, but he wasn't in.'

'And Dylan's your brother?'

'Right. He was working. But he came back to let me into his house. Thing is, I felt so edgy, you know? Couldn't settle. So I went for a wander.'

Craven laughed. 'A wander?'

'You know. I went for a walk.'

'Where to?'

'Ended up outside the theatre.'

'That's where you work, right? The Burke and Hare? Not to be confused with—'

'Aye. That's where I work. And we used a sleeping bag as a prop for the play.'

'*MacBeth MSP*, right?'

'Right. One of the sets is his house and when things go

to shit, he's all down and out and living in a tent in Birnam Wood. And there's a pillow too. So I grabbed them from the props box and thought I'd get my head down for a bit, see if a wee sleep could take the edge off how I felt.'

Craven cleared his throat. 'You went for a sleep even though there was a manhunt for you?'

'I didn't know that, did I?'

'Come on, mate. It'd be good if you could tell us something *approaching* the truth here, not this convoluted bollocks.'

'I am telling the truth! Why would I think there was a manhunt for me?' Lennon looked at Marshall, then back at Craven. 'Why was there one?'

Craven sat back, grinning wide. 'Why do you think?'

'I've no idea.'

'Because, Lennon, someone attacked your wife.'

'What?' Lennon jerked his head back. 'Someone attacked Phoebe?'

'That's right. "They" tried to murder her, yes.' Craven did rabbit ears around "they". 'It was you, wasn't it?'

'Of course it wasn't!' Lennon gritted his teeth. 'Whatever happened to my wife is *nothing* to do with me.'

'Right, sure.' Craven sniffed. 'And yet you haven't told us where you were during the attack.'

'Jesus. I didn't know she'd been attacked!'

Craven drummed his fingers on the table, acting like he was *really* impatient. 'Come on, Lennon...'

'I swear!' Lennon shifted his gaze between them, as

though trying to assess which of the pair would be a likely ally. But all he saw was two horrible bastards. 'Tell me... What happened to her?'

'Come on, Lennon, you know.' Marshall left a pause, way longer than it should've been. 'You were there.'

'I wasn't!' Lennon started shaking. Tears swelled in his eyes. Actual tears. 'Is she still alive?'

Marshall sat back and took his time. They had him. They had caught him in their web. And it had yet to dawn on Lennon. 'Someone attacked her, Lennon. Hit her with a lamp. Thought they'd killed her.'

Lennon frowned, his eyes losing their focus. 'But she's alive?'

Marshall nodded. 'She's in hospital.'

'How is she?'

'Alive. But not awake. Jennifer's at her bedside. Not that you're interested in her wellbeing.'

'Of course I am! She might be fucking someone behind my back, but...' Lennon gritted his teeth. 'Christ. Who did it?'

'Nice try.' Marshall laughed. 'It's easier on all of us if you just admit it, Lennon. It's been a long night and I could really do with my bed. How about you, Dean?'

'Same.' Craven yawned. 'Soon as this punk admits what he's done to his wife, sooner we can get home. But I'm prepared to sit here all day, if that's what it takes.'

'I didn't kill her!'

'Come on...' Marshall stared hard at him for a few long

seconds. 'Are you saying it's just a coincidence that your wife has been savagely attacked not long after you threatened to murder her?'

'This is bullshit!'

'You shouted at her loud enough for the neighbours to hear. When officers attended, you were caught on video threatening to kill her.'

'It was just a joke!'

'Just a joke.' Marshall folded his arms. 'See, I don't find that funny at all. Do you, Dean?'

Craven shook his head. 'Nope. Not in the slightest.'

'Not a joke... I just... I didn't mean it... I...' Lennon ran a hand down his face. 'Look, me and Phoebe have had plenty of shouting matches over the years. I'm not proud of it but it's a fact. But it's also a fact that I've never, *ever* laid a hand on her.'

Marshall sat back, leaning an arm on the chair back so he was twisted around. 'Where were you at the time of the attack?'

'When was it?'

'We believe it occurred at roughly ten o'clock.'

'Asleep, maybe. I don't know.'

'Around the time you were texting your wife.'

Lennon's head slumped forward.

'You were instructed not to do that, weren't you?'

'I know, but I... I wanted to make it right. She didn't have to reply, did she?'

'Thing is, all we've got from you leaving here at nine

o'clock until half past midnight, when Sergeant Rakesh Siyal found you in your theatre, is that you went to your brother's and then you went for a wander.'

'Told you. I walked to the theatre, then lay down and fell asleep.'

'Right. But you woke up, didn't you? And you fought off my colleagues, then you ran off through Edinburgh.'

'Doesn't mean I did anything, does it? Sure if I woke you up in the middle of the night, you'd be pretty spooked. Are you saying you wouldn't react like that?'

'Personally, I wouldn't try to sleep in an empty theatre after I'd tried to murder my wife.'

'I keep telling you...'

Marshall held his gaze again, but Lennon wasn't giving up any time soon. Maybe he'd underestimated him. 'I'm prepared to believe you, Lennon, just so long as you tell us the truth. Where were you, Lennon?'

'Told you. I left Dylan's and went for a walk. I don't remember where I went. My head's a bit of a mess, to be honest with you. Bit weird when the cops come into your house, you know? When they talk to you about charges and... My head's all over the place.'

'Can well imagine.' Craven rattled his thumbs on the table. A short, explosive noise that made Lennon stare at him. 'Was that walk, perchance, to a certain light shop in Duddingston?'

'No.'

'Sure about that?'

'Sure. I think I went to the city centre.'

'You think, eh? Where did you go?'

'I don't know where. A pub.'

'A pub?'

'Aye. I went in for a drink, I think. It's where I was messaging Pheebs. Then I called Dylan but he didn't answer me this time. I should've gone back to his, really, but I went to the theatre and ended up falling asleep. Like I told you.'

Craven made a note, but Marshall couldn't see what he'd written. 'Where did you go after this incident, then?'

Lennon scratched at his stubble. 'Along the A1.'

Craven narrowed his eyes. 'You mean, the road through Abbeyhill that eventually becomes London Road and terminates at the start of Princes Street?'

Lennon shook his head. 'No. The dual carriageway bit. Heading out of the city.'

Craven sighed. 'Was that you doing your *Littlest Hobo* impression? Walking to another town, whereupon an adventure would happen upon you?'

'No. I just needed to clear my head after what happened.'

'More of an *Incredible Hulk* vibe?' Craven arched an eyebrow. 'People don't want to make you angry, right? Because when you hulk out, Lennon, you smash the shite out of people with floor lamps. Then you move on to another town, whereupon another opportunity for adventure will present itself. Am I right?'

Lennon folded his arms. 'Are you going to take this seriously?'

Craven laughed. 'I will if you will. And if you tell us what you were actually doing, not this vague nonsense about drinks in pubs and walks along a dual carriageway.'

Lennon looked around the room, then rubbed at his cheek. He screwed his face tight. 'I was going to kill myself.'

Craven roared with laughter. 'Aye, pull the other one, mate. It's got bells on.'

Lennon glowered at him. 'I'm serious.'

Marshall put a hand in front of Craven. 'You were going to kill yourself?'

'I was. Planned to... to throw myself in front of a coach or a lorry.'

The room was silent.

Marshall sat there, trying to give the admission the respect it deserved.

Lennon sighed. 'Felt like the only way out. Then I wouldn't have to deal with this shite anymore. But... I couldn't do that to the driver, you know? They'd be stuck with that the rest of their lives. And the passengers. And the other drivers who'd witnessed it. Maybe someone would crash into them. I couldn't bring that on anyone, could I?'

Marshall could tell it was the truth by the look in Lennon's eyes. You couldn't fake that. Nobody could. 'What do you mean, the only way out?'

'When you lot showed up at the theatre, I totally freaked out. I don't know why I ran from your colleagues. I just did. Thought you were going to lock me up.'

'We were. Because you'd attacked her, Lennon. You ran because you knew that.'

'No!'

Marshall leaned forward and spoke in a low voice. 'And it's more than a bit suspicious that you had money and camping gear with you.'

'What?'

'Your brother had the cash. And passports. And you had all that stuff in those bags. A tent. Sleeping bags. Tinned goods. Camping stove.' Marshall laughed. 'Amazing what you can get in Asda at that time of night, really, but there you go. Enough to run away for a bit. What was the plan?'

'I didn't have a plan.'

'Okay, so just tell us what you were going to do.'

'I told you. I was thinking of killing myself.' Lennon blew air up his face. 'I called Dylan. Told him that.' He rubbed his hands up and down his face. 'Not my first time. Got into a black state when I was at uni.'

'I'm sorry to hear that.' Marshall sat back in his chair again. 'Okay, so you're telling us you walked to the A1 from the theatre because you felt like you wanted to kill yourself?'

'Right. Managed to take back roads over there. Plenty of them in Edinburgh. Walked through the Jewel and past

Dylan's.' Lennon scratched at his neck. 'And I thought if I ended it all, the world would be a lot better without me.'

'But?'

'But I called my brother. It's good having an older brother like Dylan. He's pretty wise. He suggested we go camping for a few days. Clear my head.'

'Camping in December?'

'Done it tons of times.' Lennon bit at his nails. 'Like I say, it's not the first time I've had those thoughts. Getting very cold, wet and miserable in the Highlands seems to be as good a cure as any, for me at least.'

Marshall looked over at Craven and the briefest flash of his eyebrow told him to shut the fuck up and stay that way. He focused back on Lennon and gave him a serious expression, one full of compassion. Or so he hoped. If you met them halfway, then chances were they'd work with you the rest of it. There were exceptions, obviously, but you had to offer the olive branch. 'Thank you for your honesty, Lennon.' He left another weighty pause. Time to snatch it away. 'But I don't believe you.'

Lennon slammed a fist down on the table. 'I'm telling you the truth!'

'But the facts fit a better explanation.' Marshall raised a thumb. 'One, you were released from here under investigative liberation. You were instructed not to visit your home or to communicate with your wife during a period of two weeks. Which you just admitted to breaking, by the way. You texted her and she told you where she was. At work.' He added his forefinger. 'Next, you visited her shop. And you attacked her. Thought you'd killed her, didn't you?'

'No!'

'Come on, Lennon, it's easier if you just—'

'I didn't attack her!'

Marshall added his middle finger to the other two. 'After you thought you'd killed her, it spooked you and you ran off. You thought you'd lay low in your theatre. But we found you. And you ran away again. Next thing we know, instead of contemplating suicide, you were meeting your brother at the Asda in the Jewel.' He pushed a sheet of paper across the desk. 'We've got the record of a call between you and Dylan. I suspect you sat in an empty toilet cubicle waiting for him.'

Lennon stared at the page, but it was like he was looking through the paper. He lurched forward, resting his head in his hands. 'Please... You've got to believe me...'

Marshall looked over at Craven, who was staring at his phone under the table. 'You believe him, Dean?'

'Me? No. You?'

'Nope.'

'I think *he* believes it, though.' Craven pocketed his phone. 'Psychopaths do that, though. Lie to themselves and believe it.'

'I don't think he's a psychopath, though. Probably just an angry man.'

'An angry man who's tried to kill his wife.' Craven

stared at Lennon, but he was still hiding behind his arms. 'Easier on us all if you just own up to it, Lennon. Let us all get home.' He paused. 'Come on, Lennon. Admit you did it. It'll be easier for you in the long run.'

'I didn't attack her!' Lennon sat up and wiped his fingers across his eyes. He was frowning, like he was processing some detailed information about the existence of God. 'If Phoebe was attacked...' He looked up, scowling. 'I *know* my wife has been sleeping with someone. The scumbag who was shagging her... He might've done this.'

Marshall sighed. 'That doesn't sound likely to me.'

Lennon glowered at him. 'Come on, they did it this evening in our bed.'

'When?'

'When I was in the police station.'

'You weren't there, were you?'

'No.'

'So how can you know?'

'Believe me, I *know*.'

'Come on, Lennon. You can't expect us to believe—'

'I don't know who it is, but I know she's been doing this.'

Craven smirked. 'Enlighten us, would you?'

'We've got one of those Ring doorbells. Every day, not long after I'd get to work, she'd switch it off. You don't have to guess why.' Lennon's eyes shifted between them. 'I came back early on Wednesday and caught her fiddling with it. Said the battery was broken. And she was expecting a delivery for the light shop, so she was stressed. But the bed was all crumpled. Her boyfriend was probably running over the back wall.'

'But you didn't see anyone?'

'No.'

'And what's your proof tonight?'

'The bed was crumpled. She's meticulous about it. Every morning. Did it this morning.'

'But you weren't there, were you?'

'No.'

Craven sighed. 'So you've got nothing. Just clutching at straws here.' He got up and gripped Marshall's shoulder. 'Come on, let's get him in a cell, then see how he's feeling in the a.m. Might decide to tell the truth, eh?'

Lennon looked up at him. 'I'm telling you the truth now!'

'Sure. But you have no proof of it, so I don't believe you.'

Lennon scratched at his neck. 'I might have.'

Craven laughed. 'Come on, Lennon. Evidence isn't a quantum thing that exists in a joint state of being and not being until someone looks at it. It's evidence. It either is or it isn't there. And when people say they "might" have evidence, I might be a millionaire. I'm not.'

'Listen. When Phoebe was fiddling about with the doorbell, it reminded me why I got that camera in the first place. It was so I could see who was coming to the door when we were out. And her turning it off stopped me seeing that. But it gave me an idea.' Lennon looked over at Marshall, like he was a softer target. 'The doorbell was for outside, right, but I decided to get one for inside the house.'

Marshall sat back and folded his arms. 'You set up a camera in your home?'

Lennon nodded. 'One she didn't know anything about... Points at the bedroom. So if there's some funny business going on, I'll know about it. It's a tiny thing, runs off a battery. Very hard to spot.'

'Given you know the sheets were rumpled, I'm assuming you can access it remotely?'

Lennon shook his head. 'No. It's not on wi-fi.'

'That means we need to fetch it from your home.' Marshall joined Craven standing. 'To that effect, we need you to sign a "consent to search" document for us to retrieve it.'

Lennon frowned. 'And if I don't?'

'Then we get a warrant. No big deal. Your call completely.'

Lennon scowled at them like they were thick. 'Can't you just go and get it?'

'That's what I'm talking about. A consent search. You have to be present in case you decide to revoke your consent at any time.'

'Why would I do that?'

'I don't know. Say we find a murder weapon there?'

'Fine. Give me the form and I'll show you.'

# CHAPTER THIRTY-FOUR

Rakesh stood outside the Blackwells' home on Lygon Road. The nearby lights buzzed, a white-noise symphony, but the street was otherwise quiet. Not that there was a lack of activity at quarter past four in the morning – curtains twitched in two houses over the road.

'Hard to blame them, Sarge.' Ella covered her yawn with a hand. 'Us lot showing up at the crack of sparrow fart is surely going to set tongues wagging.'

'Especially after we've already been here a few times this evening.'

'Exactly.' Ella yawned wide now. 'So bloody tired, Sarge. Should be tucked up in bed just now.'

'Tell me about it.' Rakesh looked over to the front door, hanging open to let the cold in. No sign of anyone coming back with the prize. He ran a finger across his throat but couldn't even feel where the blade had been – maybe the scars were more mental. Scratch that, it was just an idle memory now – Dylan never planned on going through with it, just a desperate man trying to protect his younger brother. 'Focus on the overtime, Ella. It'll pay towards a holiday.'

'I hate going on holiday.'

'Pay a few months of Netflix, then. Or your gym membership. Or get you some new clothes. '

'You saying I need to go to the gym?'

'No, you just look like you go.'

'Right. Was planning on going after my shift, but bugger that.' Ella blinked hard a few times. 'I'll buy some records.'

'Vinyl?'

'My dad's a massive collector. Got me addicted to it as well too. It's weird. I'm twenty-three and all I've known is music coming out of phones or speakers, right? Guess my folks must've had CDs when I was born, but it's cool to see that the actual music is a thing. You know? A disc with a C or a K that you put into or onto something and it makes the sounds.'

'Never thought of it that way. I still have the first few CDs I bought. And nobody needs to listen to that much Blink 182, do they?'

'Blink 182? You?'

'I was a massive fan. Even saw them when I was ten.'

'Bloody hell, Sarge.' Ella looked around at the house

with a grin on her face, then over at Rakesh. 'When do you think we'll get away?'

'Now Dawn's been found, night shift are taking the slack on response, which is good. Probably won't let us linger around for too long now.' Rakesh checked his watch. 'I'm waiting on a call from Asher.'

The door thudded, then Marshall charged past them, carrying a tiny device in an evidence bag.

Helen followed him, nudging Lennon in cuffs. She nodded at them as she passed, then took him over to the patrol car. Thankfully not the one with the buggered cage.

Marshall stopped and doubled back towards them. 'Rakesh, has your squad car got a laptop?'

'It does.'

'Need to borrow you, then.' Marshall looked over at the house, while Bell locked the door, then nodded at Ella. 'Check he's locked up, will you? I'll get the team to finalise the search in the morning.'

'Will do, sir.'

Rakesh led Marshall over to his squad car, then got behind the wheel. The laptop rested in a caddy between the seats, easily operable by driver or passenger, but he lifted it out and unlocked it. 'Well?'

Marshall got in the passenger seat and started fiddling with the tiny device, about the size of a postage stamp before they added QR codes and all that to them. 'Well what?'

'Were the bedsheets crumpled?'

'They were.' Marshall's giant sausage fingers were struggling with the device. 'Hard to believe this thing is a camera. But I guess that's the whole point. Stuck to the edge of a painting.' He grunted as he tried to twist it, but nothing happened. 'Sodding thi—'

Then it unclicked and slid apart.

'There we go.' Marshall popped out a Micro SD card, about the size of a child's thumbnail, and handed it over to Rakesh. 'Will that fit?'

'Think so.' Rakesh found an adaptor in the caddy's base, then eased the tiny card into it and slotted it into the side of the laptop.

The computer clicked and whirred.

On the screen, the security app appeared.

> External device scan complete.
> No known malware detected.
> Database correct at 29th November 2024.
> Proceed with transfer to secure storage? (Y/N)

Rakesh tapped the Y key.

The laptop extracted the files and flashed a folder filled with files.

> Uploading to secure cloud...

One by one, little dots were added until it read 100%.

Safe to remove.
Remember to store in evidence.

'Good machine.' Rakesh smiled as he handed back the tiny card.

Marshall slotted it back into the camera, then re-bagged it all, looking at the screen. 'Is there a timestamp?' He frowned. 'Ah, right. The filenames. Nothing since yesterday morning... Then us just now.' He pointed at a file, 20241130200513.mov. 'Okay, that one there. Today's date. Sorry. Yesterday. This evening, right?'

'Guessing it's five past eight and thirteen seconds.' Rakesh double-clicked the file and the video player opened.

On the screen, the bedroom door filled the view. Sure enough, it was timestamped 05/11/2024 20:05:13.

Rakesh hit play. The camera was in the hallway, looking across towards the bed. The hallway was silent, but the camera had been triggered by movement – shadows passed across the floor.

Phoebe appeared, leading someone by the hand. It was dark and greyscale, so they could only see his outline. Rakesh only recognised her by her clothes matching what she'd worn earlier.

She stood in the room and kissed him, his face hidden by the door.

The general shape and size had to be a man. Tall, athletic...

Hands searched across her back, caressing her arse, then started undressing her, taking time to unclasp her bra.

Then she pushed him down onto the bed with animal hunger.

The camera didn't pick up much, just showed a couple having sex in the dark. Vague shapes moving rhythmically.

Rakesh sat there, watching it and felt uncomfortable – the ultimate moment of privacy had been pricked by her husband and here they were, watching it.

She reached over and switched the light on. She was on top, riding him, his face still just off camera.

He pushed her forward and penetrated her from behind, then reached over and turned off the light.

It was dark again.

Rakesh clicked back on the timeline.

Marshall frowned at him. 'What's up?'

'Watch.'

Onscreen, Phoebe reached over again to turn on the light. Then he moved her over onto her hands and knees.

Rakesh tapped the pause button at the exact right moment.

The screen froze and the man's torso was visible in the light.

# CHAPTER THIRTY-FIVE

Rakesh drove through the security gate into the car park at the back of Craigmillar station and stopped.

A squad car sat next to Marshall's truck.

Rakesh flashed his lights at it, then drove forwards, parking so he blocked it in. He got out and walked over, then got into the passenger side. He shut the door but didn't say anything.

Bell was behind the wheel, tapping at it in time to the chart dance music playing at a low volume on the radio. 'That us finished, Sarge?'

'You locked up the house?'

'Aye. Keys are with Ella. She was putting them into storage for me.'

'Excellent. Well, the good news is DCI Marshall has signed off on OT until seven for each of us.'

Bell cracked his knuckles, then glanced at the clock. 'But we can get off shift now?'

'The rest of the team can.'

Bell scowled. 'What are you talking about, Shunty?'

Rakesh bristled at the use of his nickname. He got out his phone and held it out. 'Recognise this, Nytol?'

Bell squinted at the screen. 'What am I supposed to be looking at?'

'This is a still from a video taken yesterday evening at 8:05, as you can see from the timestamp.'

'And?'

'Notice anything?'

Bell grunted. 'It's dark.'

'Are you being deliberately obtuse?'

'No!'

'Have another look.' Rakesh thrust the face closer. 'It's you, you stupid bastard.'

'Fuck are you talking about?'

Rakesh flicked through more stills, all showing Ken Buchanan holding out his belt, drawn in ink across an adult male's back. 'Tell me that's not you, George.'

Bell sat back in his chair and snorted out a breath.

'Trouble with your tattoo is it's very distinctive, George. That's absolutely you.'

'Where'd you get that?'

'Inside the house. There's a hidden camera pointing at the bed.'

'This is total bullshit.'

'No, it's not. What it is, George, is a *disgrace*. You were supposed to be taking Phoebe around to her sister's, but you got diverted, didn't you?'

Bell looked at the screen, then at Rakesh, then back at the phone. 'That's not a crime.'

'What?'

'Come on, Sarge. I was off duty.' Bell pointed at his face. 'Broke my nose. Remember?'

'Did you go to A&E? Or did you just stay and have sex with her?'

Bell didn't say anything, just sat back and refolded his arms.

Rakesh shook his head. 'I'm giving you one opportunity here to set this right. Tell me the truth. What happened?'

'I don't have to tell you anything.'

'This isn't one of those "anything you do say" situations, George. I'm your sergeant. You owe me an explanation.' Rakesh scowled at him. 'You had sex with the victim of domestic abuse while you were on shift. Sure, you might've been told to get to A&E because of your nose, but you didn't go. You'd been entrusted with getting her to her sister's. And we found her car near the light shop, so you didn't even drive her, did you? She drove herself to her sister's, then to the shop.'

Bell thought about it for a few long seconds. 'Fuck it.' He grinned. 'You've got the hard evidence, like you say.'

'Don't joke.'

'Sorry. But there's no point in denying it.' Bell swallowed hard. 'As soon as Helen and Ella left, Phoebe said she needed to grab some clothes. So I went up there with her, just to make sure there was no funny business, you know? But she was all over me. Hands like an octopus. Kissing me like a squid.'

'And you kissed her back?'

'Well, aye. Then... It just sort of happened.'

'Just sort of happened.' Rakesh laughed, but it was like a punch. 'Then what did you do?'

'I left. Went to the big Asda in Chesser, on the other side of town, and got some gauze to make it look like I'd been to A&E.'

'Why didn't you just go?'

'Don't know, to be honest. Wish I had. Nose is fucking killing me.'

'You were driving solo after that. Did you attempt to murder her?'

'Of course not!'

'Seems like you've got a plausible motive here, George.'

'I shagged her, sure. But that's it. That's all I did. Of course I didn't kill her. And I was in the station at the time of the attack.'

'You knew her, didn't you?'

'Eh? Of course not.'

'You've been having an affair with her for weeks.'

'Have I fuck! That was the first time I met her in my puff.'

'You're saying this was just an opportunistic thing?'

'Exactly. Like I said, she pounced on me. Happens all the time, mate. You know that saying – women love a man in uniform.'

'Of course it doesn't happen all the time.'

'At least once a week.'

'You have sex with someone on duty once a week?'

'No! But they come on to me.'

'Why was this different?'

'I don't know. You're telling me no one's ever come on to you, Shunty?'

'You were doing so well there, George. Time to go back to the truth. Her husband believes she was having sex with someone. I've cross-referenced these times with your shift patterns. There are times when you were on shift when she—'

'Whoa, whoa!' Bell raised his hands. 'Listen, pal, if she's been shagging someone behind his back, sure as hell wasn't me! Apart from tonight. And I swear that's the first and only time with her. I swear. The only time.'

'Detectives will go through your movements over the last few months, George. They'll get to the actual truth.'

'What? You've reported me?'

'Not yet, but I have to.' Rakesh held his gaze until he looked away. 'George, you know I worked in Professional Standards for a while. I know a bent cop when I see one. I can smell them a mile off. Right now, you're stinking like an open tin of tuna left in the sun for a week.'

'Fuck off, you cunt! This is my job!'

'Sure, but you need to be held responsible—'

'Fuck you! You come in here, taking over and… Truth is, you're a fucking rat. You're only here to take down good cops like me.'

'Good cops don't have sex with victims, George. You know you're going to lose your job.'

'What? This is complete bullshit!'

'Do I need to quote regulations at you?'

'Fuck off.' Bell glared at him. 'Fuck you, Shunty. This is your fault.'

Rakesh laughed. 'My fault?'

'Of course it is! You're the sergeant. This is on you.'

'*You* did this, George. Not me. You. Your actions, your fault. I wish to God I'd got Ella or Helen to—'

'Prick. I'm going to talk to my federation rep about this bullshit.'

'Not stopping you.' Rakesh got out of the car and walked away towards the station.

# CHAPTER THIRTY-SIX

Rakesh sat in an interview room, a colleague on one side, opposite the suspect.

He'd missed this. That feeling of... it was hard to pin down. An adversarial challenge – the intellectual puzzle of presenting an argument based on solid evidence, coupled with the emotional exchange and having to react in real time. Reading someone's body language. Connecting with them. Forcing them in another direction than the one they planned.

The whole thing made Rakesh feel at home for the first time since he'd moved to the Craigmillar nick.

Or it would've done if his head wasn't still full of George Bell's nonsense.

He couldn't believe it.

Or he could. All too well.

Marshall nudged Rakesh's knee under the table.

Rakesh cleared his throat and focused on Lennon. 'You know we found the camera because you led us to it. And we've been through the contents.'

Lennon squirmed in his seat. 'And?'

Rakesh fiddled with some pages he had in front of him.

'What did you find? *Has* she been shagging someone?'

'We need to confirm your chain of events.'

'So you're saying she did fuck someone?'

'You said you knew she had.'

'Eh?'

'Earlier. You said you knew she'd been sleeping with someone tonight.'

'I... Right.' Lennon frowned. 'I did.'

'Is that because you went inside to check the video?'

'No.'

'I guess you can delete the files easily, right?'

'I don't know. I haven't had to yet. That thing can record for a year, give or take.'

Rakesh tapped the top sheet. 'So my question is, how did you know someone had been there with her?'

Lennon frowned. 'I guessed.'

'You guessed.' Rakesh looked over at Marshall, then back at Lennon. He laughed. 'You knew what was on that video, didn't you?'

'How could I? I hadn't been there.'

'But you still have a key to the house. After you left here, following your release, you got into a taxi. I saw it.

You could've gone home. You could've checked the camera there.'

'Could've. But I didn't.'

'Okay, we'll just take your word for it, then.'

'Mate... You should be checking in with taxi companies and so on, shouldn't you?'

'We were hoping you'd be able to just tell us the truth.'

Lennon stared down at the tabletop and rubbed at his forehead. 'Listen.' He looked up at Rakesh with a deep sadness in his eyes. 'I set up that camera days ago but it never triggered when I was out. I kept checking, but it was just stuff from when we were both in. Like this morning.'

'It triggered tonight. And you checked it. And you saw red. Then you went to the shop and killed her.'

'I didn't!'

'No. You didn't kill her. But you tried to. And you thought you'd succeeded.'

Lennon looked away and kneaded his forehead. 'Who was it?'

'Who was what?'

'On the video. Who was it? Who was fucking my wife?'

'We can't disclose that.'

'Come on. Some fucker was screwing my wife and you can't tell me?'

'That's correct. Because you've clearly got form for committing violent acts against—'

Lennon drove his fist onto the table again. 'Was it a man?'

Rakesh narrowed his eyes. 'Come on, Lennon. You've seen the video. You know who it was.'

'I haven't been inside the house. You told me not to go. I respected that.'

'I told you to not kill your wife, but that didn't stop you from trying, did it?'

Lennon sat in silence, mouth open. He started panting like a dog.

Another leg nudge from Marshall, who sat forward. 'Mr Blackwell, I'm prepared to believe you.'

Lennon frowned. At least he stopped panting. 'Good.'

'Steady on there. I said I'm *prepared* to believe you. That doesn't mean I do. Not yet, anyway. We've got a big distance to travel to get there. The bottom line, Lennon, is you need to be completely honest with us. Completely. Okay?'

'It's what I'm doing!'

'Did you watch that video file?'

'No. I didn't go back home!'

'Okay.' Marshall stroked his chin. 'So the question I have is how did you know she was sleeping with someone?'

'The Ring camera was off.'

'You checked?'

'Right. I wanted to know if Phoebe had gone. You get a notification when someone comes in or out of the house. The only thing I got was a neighbour walking past the end of our drive.'

'Were you checking so that you knew when to go back and collect the video from your interior camera?'

'No. I was going to go and get some stuff.' Lennon ran a hand across his bald scalp. 'In the end, Dylan said he'd swing by the house and pick up some clothes for me.'

Marshall frowned. 'And did he?'

'I don't know. The camera was off. It's what he said he was doing when I was out walking.'

'Where's the stuff?'

'I don't know.' Lennon's lips twitched. 'He acted weird about it.'

'Did he say anything?'

'Nothing. Just that the bedding was crumpled.'

'But you spoke to him on the phone, right?'

'Right.'

'And that's when you saw red, right? Went there and attacked—'

'No! He said we should go away.'

'Do you believe that he was there?'

'At the house?' Lennon's lips twisted up, then he let out a sigh. He frowned. 'Are you saying *he* shagged Phoebe?'

'No, he didn't.'

'You know that?'

'We do.'

'Okay, so you won't tell me who did, but you'll tell me who didn't?'

Marshall raised his hands. 'This isn't an opportunity

for you to name everyone you've ever met or heard about in the hope that we'll give you a clue as to who it actually was. But to help your case, we need proof that Dylan was there.'

Lennon sat back in his chair, looking up at the ceiling. He seemed to be tossing a few things around in his head.

Rakesh hoped they were all true, or at least the one he put voice to was.

Lennon looked right at Rakesh. Maybe he was the one he trusted. 'Dylan definitely went there. And I can prove it. He fetched some clothes for me.'

'We don't have that on your camera.'

'No. He didn't go upstairs. I had a bag packed in the utility room.'

'Why?'

'When you live with someone like Phoebe, you learn to have a swift exit plan.'

'Okay, but that doesn't prove anything.'

'He took my iPad. It's in the boot of his car.'

Rakesh had seen it – it'd been on the BWV footage. 'Did Dylan know about your hidden camera?'

'The only people who do are me, the lad who sold it to me and you lot. The only way Dylan would know is if you've told him.'

# CHAPTER THIRTY-SEVEN

Rakesh entered the station's tiny observation suite wedged between the two interview rooms.

In amongst the clutter of rubbish – who needed an ironing board in a police station? – Marshall was sitting back, drinking a coffee as he watched the screen, mounted on a desk stuffed with papers that probably went out of use just after the station opened. He looked over at Rakesh and smiled. 'Morning.'

'Is it?' Rakesh collapsed into the chair and checked his watch. 'This shift is killing me.'

'Well, it's just about over. And you've got four hours' overtime coming out of my department's budget.'

'That money will come in handy, I have to say. Need to fix my bathroom.'

'What's wrong with it?'

'Toilet won't flush.'

Marshall laughed. 'Seriously?'

'Couldn't make it up, could you?' Rakesh shrugged. 'How are they doing?'

'Just getting started.' Marshall cracked his knuckles. 'Spent ages sorting out why he's not got a lawyer despite being in the station for...' He checked his watch. 'Over three hours. And he doesn't have a good reason. Only requested a lawyer twenty minutes ago.'

Onscreen, Craven and Mukherjee were the ones interviewing Dylan.

Dylan shrugged. 'Anything I can do to help my brother.'

He was sitting next to Pete, the lawyer whose taxi Lennon had taken.

'It's not about your brother.' Craven paused. 'It's about you, Mr Blackwell.'

'Me?' Dylan looked around the room. 'What am I supposed to have done?'

Craven frowned, but it was exaggerated. 'Well, when you take a police officer at knifepoint, we tend to take it seriously.'

'That can easily be explained.'

'Oh, aye?'

'I've been having issues at night. My vision gets all misty. I tend to see things that aren't there. And those that are, I think they're something else entirely. Can lead to situations like that.'

'What did you think Sergeant Siyal was? A marauding

pirate? A poisonous snake?'

'My client will address those allegations in due course.'

'Sure he will.' Craven slid a sheet of paper across the table. 'Found these in your toilet cistern.'

Dylan stared at the page for a long time. 'What's this?'

'Sorry, it's not your toilet, it's your dear old mum's. But I don't imagine she'd have been getting up there in her condition, do you? No, I suspect someone a lot younger put them there.'

Dylan put the page down. 'Nothing to do with me.'

'We've got your prints on file, Dylan.'

'So?'

'So we'll match them to the prints left on the drugs.'

'In a toilet cistern?'

'You know as well as I do that it'd been drained. Means the fingerprints are nice and pristine. And preserved.'

Dylan stared at the pages and realised he was screwed.

Probably realised why he was being interviewed by two cops from the drugs squad rather than Marshall and Rakesh.

Dylan sat there in silence.

Rakesh took the opportunity to hand his own set of pages to Marshall. 'Got this.'

Marshall turned the volume down, then checked it over. His eyebrows raised. 'Is this legit?'

Rakesh nodded. 'It's where I've been for the last hour.'

'Wow.' Marshall folded the page. 'Do you want to hand it to them?'

'Thought you would?'

'It's your work, Rakesh. On you go.'

'If you insist.' Rakesh got up and everything hurt. Felt like he was underwater. He desperately needed his bed, not to stumble into an interview room with an attempted murderer. 'Cheers, Rob.' He left the obs suite and walked along the corridor. He took a few seconds to steady himself, then cleared his throat. All it did was dislodge something, so he hacked away at it and got it. He shook himself down, swallowed, then knocked on the door.

It took a few seconds, but a chair scraped back inside, then some heavy footsteps rumbled across the room.

The door opened and Craven looked him up and down. He stepped out, nudging the door shut behind him. 'Rakesh.' He raised his eyebrows. 'You got yourself lost in your own station?'

Rakesh held out the paper for him. 'Got this for you.'

Craven took it, then checked the page with disdain. He shifted to the next with a deep grunt. 'This is—' Then his eyes bulged. He looked away, staring into space. Then back at Rakesh. 'Do you want to present this to him?'

Rakesh frowned, expecting another wind-up. 'Are you sure?'

Craven leaned in close. 'Word is, mate, you're actually

a wolf in sheep's clothing.' He thumbed behind him at the door. 'You're welcome to sink your fangs into this punk.'

Craven opened the door and slipped inside.

Rakesh grabbed the handle and followed him in.

Dylan looked up at Rakesh, then frowned.

Craven sat down next to Mukherjee and leaned in close to the microphone. 'Sergeant Rakesh Siyal has entered the room.'

Rakesh stood at the side of the table, between Dylan and Mukherjee.

Craven nodded at the page, then beckoned with his hands.

Rakesh slid a sheet of paper across the table to Dylan. He cleared his throat again but mercifully nothing came up this time.

Dylan casually looked at it. Then frowned. 'What's this supposed to be?'

'It's called evidence.' Rakesh tapped the page. 'Earlier, we had assumed you were picking up your brother, but now we know you didn't. You know that phrase – if you assume, you make an "ass" out of you and me?' He smiled. 'Well, I always check the facts. That's a list of fares one of your colleagues did yesterday evening and it shows your brother being collected from outside here, then dropped off at your home.'

'Fine.' Dylan sat back. 'And what's the relevance?'

'It tallies with both of your stories.' Rakesh slid another page over the table, the one Marshall had folded.

'This is where things start to diverge. That's a list of *your* fares for last night.'

Dylan glanced at it. 'And?'

'And it's clear from that how you couldn't have collected Lennon because you were otherwise busy.'

'I told you that.'

'You might've told us that you were busy, sure, but you didn't tell us where you were.' Rakesh tapped the page. 'Because at that time, you were collecting a fare from Sheridan Lights.'

Dylan shrugged. 'Right.'

'Who was it?'

'I think I was picking up Jennifer Sheridan.'

Rakesh raised his eyebrows. 'You think?'

'I know.'

'Jennifer is Phoebe's sister.' Rakesh smiled. 'Weird how she didn't mention that. And even weirder how you didn't, either.'

'Why would she?'

'Because she mentioned that you're acquainted. And a bit more than acquainted, I believe?'

'What are you talking about?'

'If I was picked up by an ex-boyfriend, I'd remember. And I'd tell the police when I spoke to them about it. But neither you nor Jennifer seemed to want to raise that point with us.'

'Are you saying I've lied to you?'

'You can lie by telling us something that's not true.

But you can also lie by hiding something from us that *is* true. Something you might not want us to know. And, of course, you can do both. You can lie to our face about stuff and you can deflect other things.'

Dylan sat back, scowling. 'You think I did something to her?'

'To Jennifer? No. We believe you. I just spoke to her on the phone.' Rakesh handed over another page. 'She's just confirmed it. Even apologised for omitting that from her statement.' He pointed at the sheet. 'But how do you explain returning to the shop ten minutes later?'

Dylan checked the page again. 'Must've had a fare.'

'You didn't. We know you didn't.'

Dylan sat back. He looked up at the ceiling.

'You went back and attacked Phoebe, didn't you?' Rakesh leaned against the table. 'You thought you'd killed her, right? And it turned out you didn't. When you learned that fact, you thought it'd be better to frame your brother for it.'

Dylan scratched at his head. 'What do you want from me?'

'The truth would be a good place to start.'

Dylan shot him a glare, but it soon faded. He looked down, staring at the table. 'Lennon told me Phoebe was talking to the cops. I thought it was...'

'Thought it was what?'

'Another matter. Something you don't need to worry yourself about.'

Craven perked up at that. 'You're talking about the drugs, right?'

Dylan kept staring at the wood.

Rakesh stood up tall. 'You drove there and you confronted Phoebe, didn't you? Thought she was talking to us about the drugs you'd been storing at the shop. And the cash you'd been putting through the till. Then, when she didn't respond, you decided to kill her.'

'Except she didn't die.' Craven leaned forward. 'She's in hospital, isn't she? She's awake now and my team are waiting to speak to her.' He left a pause. 'Come on, Dylan, time for the truth. Why did you try to kill her?'

Dylan shut his eyes.

Craven laughed. 'You must know you're deep in trouble here, Dylan. Even your lawyer here's not biting. The best thing for you is if you just tell us what happened.'

Dylan looked right at him. 'You want the truth? Fuck it. Way I see it, I'm screwed six ways to Sunday.' He snarled, then took a deep breath. 'Like he said, Jennifer was laundering money for me. And storing drugs.' He picked up the piece of paper, crumpled it up, then threw it over to Craven. 'That light shop was struggling. Badly. They were close to going to the wall. Three generations or something. Don't get me wrong, Phoebe's a good person but she's got *no* idea how to run a business. Thinks she does but wouldn't listen. And Jen could see just how screwed they were. I had a ton of cash I needed to clean, so she put it through the till for me.' He scratched his neck. 'I work at the school around the corner, so I'd pop into the shop to speak to Jen at lunchtime when Phoebe was having hers back at the house. Me and Jen would stick a bunch of transactions through the till. Put myself up as a fake supplier of lights. Pretended I was based in Copenhagen. In Denmark. Like I was the UK arm. So I'd send them stock and they'd sell it. Not a *lot* of money, but enough for me. And it was more than enough for her. For them. Then she started storing drugs for me there. Same at her house.'

'Phoebe's house?'

'Right. They were in boxes of lights. Massive bags of weed and a bit of coke. Enough to weigh the same as a light. Jen persuaded her that I knew the supplier, so I'd go around after work and pick it up. After my brother left for work. And he got a bit suspicious. Started asking me all these questions about Phoebe. What she was up to. Thinking she was having an affair.'

'Did you have sex with her?'

'With *Phoebe*?'

'Yes. Did you fuck her?'

'No, she's my sister-in-law!'

'It does happen.'

'Not to us. God, no!'

'So you were just there to store drugs?'

'Right. Mum finally went into a home last week. So I took the gear from theirs and hid it in the toilet cistern.'

'Might not have had sex with her but you tried to kill her.'

Dylan shrugged. 'Lennon said she was talking to the cops. Jen said some came around to hers. I put two and two together.'

'And you got fifty-seven million times pi to the power of a billion.'

'Say what you want, but I'll still win.' Dylan smiled at them. 'You want to know how I got the money out of this fake importer? I put it all into Bitcoin and hid it where you'll never find it. It's all mine and you mendacious fucks can't get at it. When I'm out of prison, I'll still have it.'

Craven looked like he was going to punch the table. He stood up tall and checked with Mukherjee. Then focused on Dylan. 'Dylan Blackwell, I'm arresting you for the attempted murder of—'

# CHAPTER THIRTY-EIGHT

Marshall hadn't slept in close to twenty-four hours and it felt like twice that. The daylight hurt his eyes, even though it was a thin dreich out there. First of December – where had the year gone?

Hamish Asher was a curious-looking man. His thick forehead made him look like an alien in *Star Trek*, but he wasn't to be underestimated. He was sharp and sleekit with it.

They stood in the doorway of the hospital room, looking in through the window.

Phoebe lay on the bed, barely awake. Not making eye contact with anyone.

Jennifer sat next to her, looking up at Rakesh and Helen. 'What?'

Helen cleared her throat. 'I said, I'm arresting you for the crime of—'

'I heard you, but what the fuck?' Jennifer looked around the room. 'Drug dealing? What are you talking about?'

'And money laundering, too. You need to come with us.'

'Going nowhere while my sister's like this!'

'It wasn't a request.'

Asher stepped away from the door, leading Marshall away. 'Wasn't even shagging her.' He shook his head as they walked. 'Think you've seen everything in this game, don't you?'

Marshall nodded. 'Constantly surprises me.'

'And they reckon he'll get away with that money?'

'Craven said they'll keep searching, but the problem with cryptocurrencies is it's a good way to store illicit gains, just so long as you're very careful about it. They reckon he's got about a hundred grand's worth. By the time Dylan's out, it could be worth five hundred grand or five quid.'

'Still. It's quite a smart racket.'

'Indeed.'

'How long do you reckon he'll get?'

'Ten years?'

Asher blew out air. 'With the way the courts and prisons are, he'll be lucky to serve three. Then he'll be out with all that filthy lucre.' He stuffed his hands deep into his pockets. 'You heading home soon?'

'Wish I was. Got to hand over to the Edinburgh MIT's SIO.'

Asher frowned. 'Who's the SIO? Not the golden boy, is it?'

'Wouldn't know if it was.'

'Well, good luck if it is. He's a total bell end.'

'I need all the luck I can get, to be honest. Going to be a long meeting. Not like I don't have my own work to do, eh?'

'Tell me about it, Rob. I've got a ton of paperwork to get through before I can bugger off. All thanks to Rakesh reporting Bell to his old mates in Standards. The fed rep is in busting my balls, but Jesus... Bell... What a stupid twat. He'll be losing his job over a shag.'

'I've seen worse.'

'*How?*'

Marshall laughed. 'You don't want to know. What happens in Brentford, stays in Brentford.'

'Take your word for it, mate.' Asher patted Marshall on the shoulder. 'Anyway, I'll let you get on. But we should discuss your request to bring Rakesh back down to the Borders ahead of schedule.'

Marshall stared at him for a few seconds. 'You got a replacement in mind?'

'Helen Taylor has passed her sergeant's exams.'

'Yeah, but you can't promote and leave in place. Too many people know where you've buried your bodies.'

'You're right. Just have to take whatever sod grabs stripes next. It's a total crap shoot.'

'Well, I just spoke to the boss and I think we can forget that.'

Asher sniffed. 'Really?'

'For a while, at least. Rakesh's stint in uniform is helping round him out.'

Asher raised his eyebrows. 'But you're still going to take him?'

# AFTERWORD

This book shouldn't really exist, to be honest.

The reason it does is I had such a hell of a time writing the sixth Marshall book, *His Path of Darkness*, that I decided to try an experiment to improve my writing method. Something I continually do to keep myself motivated.

Previously, I would sketch out a detailed outline on cards (or the electronic equivalent), which could sometimes run to 22,000 words (the first Marshall book) or 35,000 (a secret book I haven't announced). After several rounds of edits, it'd be ready to convert into a narrative.

But I'd still get into problems with them, usually around the end of the book, as I was spending too much time in the wood and didn't notice all the trees. Or too much time in the trees and didn't notice I was in a wood. Not sure which. Anyway, I'd have massaged the early chapters and neglected the later ones to the extent where the flow at the end was poor, meaning I'd have to stop and think it through. Which slows me down. And then when I was writing and editing, so much of my focus would be on the story stuff that the line-level editing would need another pass or two.

So, I'd heard from another writer (a *Sunday Times* number one bestseller, no less) who writes his books as a screenplay first and I thought I'd try that on something easily contained to see how it would work for a full-length book, say, the next Marshall. And that's this.

*False Dawn.*

Sorry for the pun in the title. It was an accident. Honest.

Screenwriting is something I've wanted to get into and my style has been consciously in that vein – you could take any of, say, the Marshall books and easily convert that to a shootable screenplay. Whether anyone would is another matter!

But that's only part of it. I've written rather a lot of books in the mystery genre of police procedurals, I wanted to do something a wee bit different, hence putting Shunty in uniform. Note that it's not *back* in uniform as it's something he's never been. It was supposed to be his first day, but I did that with *False Start*, so it evolved as I planned it. And hopefully he has evolved too – he's not the same green-around-the-gills loveable numpty as in that story; his tenure in the Borders MIT and in Professional Standards & Ethics, as well as his brief stint in uniform, has let him develop into a rounded officer.

And writing a story where the prologue bit happens near the middle was something that interested me too – how to make that first chunk interesting without the crutch to rely on. And hopefully I've captured the chaos of a uniform back shift. And writing about Edinburgh again... Man, I've missed the place...

The editing process for this has been a *lot* easier, mainly because it happened on a 22,000-word screenplay, which is a linear story that's easy to parse and process, but also significantly easier to change without rich descriptions ballsing everything up! The editing of the novel would've been even easier had (either) I read an edit note more clearly (or my editor expressed it more clearly. I still think I'm right). I think where we've got to with this makes the story much stronger.

So, that's *False Dawn* and hopefully you'll enjoy it when it comes out. It was really fun to write and it's given me a new level of enthusiasm for future books. And I really love the characters here. Maybe some will come back in future.

Now, on to edit something else and to start work on *Fear of Any Kind*, Marshall 7...

And there might, just might, be another Shunty book coming, provisionally entitled *False Hope*...

As ever, thanks to James Mackay for the help with the early work up to editing. All those drafts of the synopsis, the screenplay and the first draft of the novel felt less like a kick in the teeth for me. And to John Rickards and Julia Gibbs, as ever, for their copy editing and proofing. All mistakes in this are mine. Also, thanks to Angus King for narrating these books.

As ever, please leave a review or a rating on Amazon and I'd appreciate it – it really does help.

Ed James
　Scottish Borders, September 2024

# RAKESH WILL RETURN IN

**False Hope**

*Early 2025*

Sign up to my mailing list to be first to know when it's out...

Sign up for FREE and get access to exclusive content and keep up-to-speed with all of my releases on a monthly basis:

https://geni.us/EJM1FS

# ABOUT THE AUTHOR

**Ed James** is a Scottish author who writes crime fiction novels across multiple series and in multiple locations.

His latest series is set in the Scottish Borders, where Ed now lives, starring **DI Rob Marshall** – a criminal profiler turned detective, investigating serial murders in a beautiful landscape.

Set four hundred miles south on the gritty streets of East London, his bestselling **DI Fenchurch** series features a cop with little to lose and a kidnapped daughter to find..

His **Police Scotland** books are fronted by multiple detectives based in Edinburgh, including **Scott Cullen**, a young Edinburgh Detective investigating crimes from the bottom rung of the career ladder he's desperate to climb, and **Craig Hunter**, a detective shoved back into uniform who struggles to overcome his PTSD from his time in the army.

Putting Dundee on the tartan noir map, the **DS Vicky Dodds** books feature a driven female detective struggling to combine her complex home life with a heavy caseload.

Formerly an IT project manager, Ed filled his weekly commute to London by writing on planes, trains and automobiles. He now writes full-time and lives in the Scottish Borders with a menagerie of rescued animals.

Connect with Ed online:

Amazon Author page

Website

Printed in Great Britain
by Amazon